Stories of Friends and Enemies

Who
Do You Think
You Are?

Selected by

Hazel Rochman *and* Darlene Z. McCampbell

Little, Brown and Company

Boston   Toronto   London

Copyright acknowledgments appear on page 169.

ISBN 0-316-75355-6
Library of Congress Catalog Card Number 93-314

Joy Street Books are published by Little, Brown and Company (Inc.)

10 9 8 7 6 5 4 3 2 1

RRD-VA

Published simultaneously in Canada by
Little, Brown & Company (Canada) Limited

Printed in the United States of America

I loved my friend.
He went away from me.
There's nothing more to say.
The poem ends,
Soft as it began —
I loved my friend.

Langston Hughes

Contents

Introduction

Sometimes you need a good friend just to get through the school day.

The stories in this collection show how love and hurt get all mixed up, how you make friends and lose them and sometimes keep them for a lifetime. A friend you've grown up with moves away. You find a friend in your family. You've hurt someone who depends on you, and you wish you could go back and put things right. You share good times, danger, secrets. Someone you laughed with is now laughing at you. A friend lets you down. Or throws you a lifeline. Or transforms you.

Is it fiend or friend who lures you over the threshold of your parents' kitchen door? Is it friend or enemy who exposes you to a dark corner inside yourself? Friends make you brave and help you know who you are.

A friend — like a good story — can make the world bigger.

Good Grief

from *Dandelion Wine*

Ray Bradbury

The facts about John Huff, aged twelve, are simple and soon stated. He could pathfind more trails than any Choctaw or Cherokee since time began, could leap from the sky like a chimpanzee from a vine, could live underwater two minutes and slide fifty yards downstream from where you last saw him. The baseballs you pitched him he hit in the apple trees, knocking down harvests. He could jump six-foot orchard walls, swing up branches faster and come down, fat with peaches, quicker than anyone else in the gang. He ran laughing. He sat easy. He was not a bully. He was kind. His hair was dark and curly and his teeth were white as cream. He remembered the words to all the cowboy songs and would teach you if you asked. He knew the names of all the wild flowers and when the moon would rise and set and when the tides came in or out. He was, in fact, the only god living in the whole of Green Town, Illinois, during the twentieth century that Douglas Spaulding knew of.

And right now he and Douglas were hiking out beyond town on another warm and marble-round day, the sky blue blown-glass reaching high, the creeks bright with mirror waters fanning over white stones. It was a day as perfect as the flame of a candle.

Douglas walked through it thinking it would go on this way forever. The perfection, the roundness, the grass smell traveled on out ahead as far and fast as the speed of light. The sound of a good friend whistling like an oriole, pegging the softball, as you horse-danced, key-jingled the dusty paths, all of it was complete, everything could be touched; things stayed near, things were at hand and would remain.

It was such a fine day and then suddenly a cloud crossed the sky, covered the sun, and did not move again.

John Huff had been speaking quietly for several minutes. Now Douglas stopped on the path and looked over at him.

"John, say that again."

"You heard me the first time, Doug."

"Did you say you were — going away?"

"Got my train ticket here in my pocket. Whoo-whoo, clang! Shush-shush-shush-shush. Whooooooooo . . . "

His voice faded.

John took the yellow and green train ticket solemnly from his pocket and they both looked at it.

"Tonight!" said Douglas. "My gosh! Tonight we were going to play Red Light, Green Light and Statues! How come, all of a sudden? You been here in Green Town all my life. You just don't pick up and leave!"

"It's my father," said John. "He's got a job in Milwaukee. We weren't sure until today . . ."

"My gosh, here it is with the Baptist picnic next week and the big carnival Labor Day and Halloween — can't your dad wait till then?"

John shook his head.

"Good grief!" said Douglas. "Let me sit down!"

They sat under an old oak tree on the side of the hill looking back at town, and the sun made large trembling shadows around them; it was cool as a cave in under the tree. Out beyond, in sunlight, the town was painted with heat, the windows all gaping. Douglas wanted to run back in there where the town, by its very weight, its houses, their bulk, might enclose and prevent John's ever getting up and running off.

"But we're friends," Douglas said helplessly.

"We always will be," said John.

"You'll come back to visit every *week* or so, won't you?"

"Dad says only once or twice a year. It's eighty miles."

"Eighty miles ain't far!" shouted Douglas.

"No, it's not far at all," said John.

"My grandma's got a phone. I'll call you. Or maybe we'll all visit up your way, too. That'd be great!"

John said nothing for a long while.

"Well," said Douglas, "let's talk about something."

"What?"

"My gosh, if you're going away, we got a million things to talk about! All the things we would've talked about next month, the month after! Praying mantises, zeppelins, acrobats, sword swallowers! Go on like you was back there, grasshoppers spitting tobacco!"

"Funny thing is I don't feel like talking about grasshoppers."

"You always did!"

"Sure." John looked steadily at the town. "But I guess this just ain't the time."

"John, what's wrong? You look funny . . ."

John had closed his eyes and screwed up his face. "Doug, the Terle house, upstairs, you know?"

"Sure."

"The colored windowpanes on the little round windows, have they *always* been there?"

"Sure."

"You *positive?*"

"Darned old windows been there since before we were born. Why?"

"I never saw them before today," said John. "On the way walking through town I looked up and there they were. Doug, what was I *doing* all these years I didn't see them?"

"You had other things to do."

"Did I?" John turned and looked in a kind of panic at Douglas. "Gosh, Doug, why should those darn windows scare me? I mean, that's nothing to be scared of, is it? It's just . . ." He floundered. "It's just, if I didn't see those windows until today, what *else* did I miss? And what about all the things I *did* see here in town? Will I be able to remember them when I go away?"

"Anything you want to remember, you remember. I went to camp two summers ago. Up *there* I remembered."

"No, you didn't! You told me. You woke nights and couldn't remember your mother's face."

"*No!*"

"Some nights it happens to me in my own house; scares heck out of me. I got to go in my folks' room and look at their faces while they sleep, to be sure! And I go back to my room and lose it again. Gosh, Doug, oh gosh!" He held onto his knees tight. "Promise me just one thing, Doug. Promise you'll remember me, promise you'll remember my face and everything. Will you promise?"

"Easy as pie. Got a motion-picture machine in my head. Lying in bed nights I can just turn on a light in my head and out it comes on the wall, clear as heck, and there you'll be, yelling and waving at me."

"Shut your eyes, Doug. Now, tell me, what color eyes I got? Don't peek. What color eyes I got?"

Douglas began to sweat. His eyelids twitched nervously.

"Aw heck, John, that's not fair."

"Tell me!"

"Brown!"

John turned away. "No, sir."

"What you mean, no?"

"You're not even close!" John closed his eyes.

"Turn around here," said Douglas. "Open up, let me see."

"It's no use," said John. "You forgot already. Just the way I said."

"Turn around here!" Douglas grabbed him by the hair and turned him slowly.

"Okay, Doug."

John opened his eyes.

"Green." Douglas, dismayed, let his hand drop. "Your eyes are green . . . Well, that's close to brown. Almost hazel!"

"Doug, don't lie to me."

"All right," said Doug quietly. "I won't."

They sat there listening to the other boys running up the hill, shrieking and yelling at them.

They raced along the railroad tracks, opened their lunch in brown-paper sacks, and sniffed deeply of the wax-wrapped deviled-ham sandwiches and green-sea pickles and colored peppermints. They ran and ran again and Douglas bent to scorch his ear on the hot steel rails, hearing trains so far away they were unseen voyagings in other lands, sending Morse-code messages to him here under the killing sun. Douglas stood up, stunned.

"John!"

For John was running, and this was terrible. Because if you ran, time ran. You yelled and screamed and raced and rolled and tumbled and all of a sudden the sun was gone and the whistle was blowing and you were on your long way home to supper. When you weren't looking, the sun got around behind you! The only way to keep things slow was to watch everything and do nothing! You could stretch a day to three days, sure, just by watching!

"John!"

There was no way to get him to help now, save by a trick.

"John, ditch, ditch the others!"

Yelling, Douglas and John sprinted off, kiting the wind downhill, letting gravity work for them, over meadows, around barns until at last the sound of the pursuers faded.

John and Douglas climbed into a haystack which was like a great bonfire crisping under them.

"Let's not do anything," said John.

"Just what I was going to say," said Douglas.

They sat quietly, getting their breath.

There was a small sound like an insect in the hay.

They both heard it, but they didn't look at the sound. When Douglas moved his wrist the sound ticked in another part of the haystack. When he brought his arm around on his lap the sound ticked in his lap. He let his eyes fall in a brief flicker. The watch said three o'clock.

Douglas moved his right hand stealthily to the ticking, pulled out the watch stem. He set the hands back.

Now they had all the time they would ever need to look long and close at the world, feel the sun move like a fiery wind over the sky.

But at last John must have felt the bodiless weight of their shadows shift and lean, and he spoke.

"Doug, what time is it?"

"Two-thirty."

John looked at the sky.

Don't! thought Douglas.

"Looks more like three-thirty, four," said John. "Boy Scout. You learn them things."

Douglas sighed and slowly turned the watch ahead.

John watched him do this, silently. Douglas looked up. John punched him, not hard at all, in the arm.

With a swift stroke, a plunge, a train came and went so quickly the boys all leapt aside, yelling, shaking their fists after it, Douglas and John with them. The train roared down the track, two hundred people in it, gone. The dust followed it a little way toward the south, then settled in the golden silence among the blue rails.

The boys were walking home.

"I'm going to Cincinnati when I'm seventeen and be a railroad fireman," said Charlie Woodman.

"I got an uncle in New York," said Jim. "I'll go there and be a printer."

Doug did not ask the others. Already the trains were chanting and he saw their faces drifting off on back observation platforms, or pressed to windows. One by one they slid away. And then the empty track and the summer sky and himself on another train run in another direction.

Douglas felt the earth move under his feet and saw their shadows move off the grass and color the air.

He swallowed hard, then gave a screaming yell, pulled back his fist, shot the indoor ball whistling in the sky. "Last one home's a rhino's behind!"

They pounded down the tracks, laughing, flailing the air.

There went John Huff, not touching the ground at all. And here came Douglas, touching it all the time.

It was seven o'clock, supper over, and the boys gathering one by one from the sound of their house doors slammed and their parents crying to them not to slam the doors. Douglas and Tom and Charlie and John stood among half a dozen others and it was time for hide-and-seek and Statues.

"Just one game," said John. "Then I got to go home. The train leaves at nine. Who's going to be 'it'?"

"Me," said Douglas.

"That's the first time I ever heard of anybody volunteering to be 'it,' " said Tom.

Douglas looked at John for a long moment. "Start running," he said.

The boys scattered, yelling. John backed away, then turned and began to lope. Douglas counted slowly. He let them run far, spread out, separate each to his own small world. When they had got their momentum up and were almost out of sight, he took a deep breath.

"Statues!"

Everyone froze.

Very quietly Douglas moved across the lawn to where John Huff stood like an iron deer in the twilight.

Far away, the other boys stood hands up, faces grimaced, eyes bright as stuffed squirrels.

But here was John, alone and motionless and no one rushing or making a great outcry to spoil this moment.

Douglas walked around the statue one way, walked around the statue the other way. The statue did not move. It did not speak. It looked at the horizon, its mouth half smiling.

It was like that time years ago in Chicago when they had visited a big place where the carved marble figures were, and his walking around among them in the silence. So here was John Huff with grass stains on his knees and the seat of his pants, and cuts on his fingers and scabs on his elbows. Here was John Huff with the quiet tennis shoes, his feet sheathed in silence. There was the mouth that had chewed many an apricot pie come summer, and said many a quiet thing or two about life and the lay of the land. And there were the eyes, not blind like statues' eyes, but filled with molten green-gold. And there the dark hair blowing now north now south or any direction in the little breeze there was. And there the hands with all the town on them, dirt from roads and bark-slivers from trees, the fingers that smelled of hemp and vine and green apple, old coins or pickle-green frogs. There were the ears with the sunlight shining through them like bright warm peach wax and here, invisible, his spearmint-breath upon the air.

"John, now," said Douglas, "don't you move so much as an eyelash. I absolutely command you to stay here and not move at all for the next three hours!"

"Doug . . ."

John's lips moved.

"Freeze!" said Douglas.

John went back to looking at the sky, but he was not smiling now.

"I got to go," he whispered.

"Not a muscle, it's the game!"

"I just got to get home now," said John.

Now the statue moved, took its hands down out of the air and turned its head to look at Douglas. They stood looking at each other. The other kids were putting their arms down, too.

"We'll play one more round," said John, "except this time, I'm 'it.' Run!"

The boys ran.

"Freeze!"

The boys froze, Douglas with them.

"Not a muscle!" shouted John. "Not a hair!"

He came and stood by Douglas.

"Boy, this is the only way to do it," he said.

Douglas looked off at the twilight sky.

"Frozen statues, every single one of you, the next three minutes!" said John.

Douglas felt John walking around him even as he had walked around John a moment ago. He felt John sock him on the arm once, not too hard. "So long," he said.

Then there was a rushing sound and he knew without looking that there was nobody behind him now.

Far away, a train whistle sounded.

Douglas stood that way for a full minute, waiting for the sound of the running to fade, but it did not stop. He's still running away, but he doesn't sound any farther off, thought Douglas. Why doesn't he stop running?

And then he realized it was only the sound of his heart in his body.

Stop! He jerked his hand to his chest. Stop running! I don't *like* that sound!

And then he felt himself walking across the lawns among all the other statues now, and whether they, too, were coming to life he did not know. They did not seem to be moving at all. For that matter he himself was only moving from the knees down. The rest of him was cold stone, and very heavy.

Going up the front porch of his house, he turned suddenly to look at the lawns behind him.

The lawns were empty.

A series of rifle shots. Screen doors banged one after the other, a sunset volley, along the street.

Statues are best, he thought. They're the only things you can keep on your lawn. Don't ever let them move. Once you do, you can't do a thing with them.

Suddenly his fist shot out like a piston from his side and it shook itself hard at the lawns and the street and the gathering dusk. His face was choked with blood, his eyes were blazing.

"John!" he cried. "You, John! John, you're my enemy, you hear? You're no friend of mine! Don't come back now, ever! Get away, you! Enemy, you hear? That's what you are! It's all off between us, you're dirt, that's all, dirt! John, you hear me, John!"

As if a wick had been turned a little lower in a great clear lamp beyond the town, the sky darkened still more. He stood on the porch, his mouth gasping and working. His fist still thrust straight out at that house across the street and down the way. He looked at the fist and it dissolved, the world dissolved beyond it.

Going upstairs, in the dark, where he could only feel his face but see nothing of himself, not even his fists, he told himself over and over, I'm mad, I'm angry, I hate him, I'm mad, I'm angry, I hate him!

Ten minutes later, slowly he reached the top of the stairs, in the dark . . .

Where Are You Going, Where Have You Been?

Joyce Carol Oates

to Bob Dylan

Her name was Connie. She was fifteen and she had a quick nervous giggling habit of craning her neck to glance into mirrors, or checking other people's faces to make sure her own was all right. Her mother, who noticed everything and knew everything and who hadn't much reason any longer to look at her own face, always scolded Connie about it. "Stop gawking at yourself, who are you? You think you're so pretty?" she would say. Connie would raise her eyebrows at these familiar complaints and look right through her mother, into a shadowy vision of herself as she was right at that moment: she knew she was pretty and that was everything. Her mother had been pretty once too, if you could believe those old snapshots in the album, but now her looks were gone and that was why she was always after Connie.

"Why don't you keep your room clean like your sister? How've you got your hair fixed — what the hell stinks? Hair spray? You don't see your sister using that junk."

Her sister June was twenty-four and still lived at home. She was a secretary in the high school Connie attended, and if that wasn't bad enough — with her in the same building —

she was so plain and chunky and steady that Connie had to hear her praised all the time by her mother and her mother's sisters. June did this, June did that, she saved money and helped clean the house and cooked and Connie couldn't do a thing, her mind was all filled with trashy daydreams. Their father was away at work most of the time and when he came home he wanted supper and he read the newspaper at supper and after supper he went to bed. He didn't bother talking much to them, but around his bent head Connie's mother kept picking at her until Connie wished her mother were dead and she herself were dead and it were all over. "She makes me want to throw up sometimes," she complained to her friends. She had a high, breathless, amused voice which made everything she said sound a little forced, whether it was sincere or not.

There was one good thing: June went places with girlfriends of hers, girls who were just as plain and steady as she, and so when Connie wanted to do that her mother had no objections. The father of Connie's best girlfriend drove the girls the three miles to town and left them off at a shopping plaza, so that they could walk through the stores or go to a movie, and when he came to pick them up again at eleven he never bothered to ask what they had done.

They must have been familiar sights, walking around that shopping plaza in their shorts and flat ballerina slippers that always scuffed the sidewalk, with charm bracelets jingling on their thin wrists; they would lean together to whisper and laugh secretly if someone passed by who amused or interested them. Connie had long dark blond hair that drew anyone's eye to it, and she wore part of it pulled up on her head and puffed out and the rest of it she let fall down her back. She wore a pullover jersey blouse that looked one way when she was at home and another way when she was away from home.

Everything about her had two sides to it, one for home and
one for anywhere that was not home: her walk that could be
childlike and bobbing, or languid enough to make anyone
think she was hearing music in her head, her mouth which
was pale and smirking most of the time, but bright and pink
on these evenings out, her laugh which was cynical and
drawling at home — "Ha, ha, very funny" — but high-
pitched and nervous anywhere else, like the jingling of the
charms on her bracelet.

Sometimes they did go shopping or to a movie, but sometimes they went across the highway, ducking fast across the
busy road, to a drive-in restaurant where older kids hung
out. The restaurant was shaped like a big bottle, though
squatter than a real bottle, and on its cap was a revolving
figure of a grinning boy who held a hamburger aloft. One
night in midsummer they ran across, breathless with daring,
and right away someone leaned out a car window and invited
them over, but it was just a boy from high school they didn't
like. It made them feel good to be able to ignore him. They
went up through the maze of parked and cruising cars to
the bright-lit, fly-infested restaurant, their faces pleased and
expectant as if they were entering a sacred building that
loomed out of the night to give them what haven and what
blessing they yearned for. They sat at the counter and crossed
their legs at the ankles, their thin shoulders rigid with excite-
ment, and listened to the music that made everything so
good: the music was always in the background like music at
a church service, it was something to depend upon.

A boy named Eddie came in to talk with them. He sat
backward on his stool, turning himself jerkily around in semi-
circles and then stopping and turning again, and after awhile
he asked Connie if she would like something to eat. She said
she did and so she tapped her friend's arm on her way out —

her friend pulled her face up into a brave droll look — and Connie said she would meet her at eleven, across the way. "I just hate to leave her like that," Connie said earnestly, but the boy said that she wouldn't be alone for long. So they went out to his car and on the way Connie couldn't help but let her eyes wander over the windshields and faces all around her, her face gleaming with a joy that had nothing to do with Eddie or even this place; it might have been the music. She drew her shoulders up and sucked in her breath with the pure pleasure of being alive, and just at that moment she happened to glance at a face just a few feet from hers. It was a boy with shaggy black hair, in a convertible jalopy painted gold. He stared at her and then his lips widened into a grin. Connie slit her eyes at him and turned away, but she couldn't help glancing back and there he was still watching her. He wagged a finger and laughed and said, "Gonna get you, baby," and Connie turned away again without Eddie noticing anything.

She spent three hours with him, at the restaurant where they ate hamburgers and drank Cokes in wax cups that were always sweating, and then down an alley a mile or so away, and when he left her off at five to eleven only the movie house was still open at the plaza. Her girlfriend was there, talking with a boy. When Connie came up the two girls smiled at each other and Connie said, "How was the movie?" and the girl said, "*You* should know." They rode off with the girl's father, sleepy and pleased, and Connie couldn't help but look at the darkened shopping plaza with its big empty parking lot and its signs that were faded and ghostly now, and over at the drive-in restaurant where cars were still circling tirelessly. She couldn't hear the music at this distance.

Next morning June asked her how the movie was and Connie said, "So-so."

She and that girl and occasionally another girl went out

several times a week that way, and the rest of the time Connie spent around the house — it was summer vacation — getting in her mother's way and thinking, dreaming, about the boys she met. But all the boys fell back and dissolved into a single face that was not even a face, but an idea, a feeling, mixed up with the urgent insistent pounding of the music and the humid night air of July. Connie's mother kept dragging her back to the daylight by finding things for her to do or saying, suddenly, "What's this about the Pettinger girl?"

And Connie would say nervously, "Oh, her. That dope." She always drew thick clear lines between herself and such girls, and her mother was simple and kindly enough to believe her. Her mother was so simple, Connie thought, that it was maybe cruel to fool her so much. Her mother went scuffling around the house in old bedroom slippers and complained over the telephone to one sister about the other, then the other called up and the two of them complained about the third one. If June's name was mentioned her mother's tone was approving, and if Connie's name was mentioned it was disapproving. This did not really mean she disliked Connie and actually Connie thought that her mother preferred her to June because she was prettier, but the two of them kept up a pretense of exasperation, a sense that they were tugging and struggling over something of little value to either of them. Sometimes, over coffee, they were almost friends, but something would come up — some vexation that was like a fly buzzing suddenly around their heads — and their faces went hard with contempt.

One Sunday Connie got up at eleven — none of them bothered with church — and washed her hair so that it could dry all day long, in the sun. Her parents and sisters were going to a barbecue at an aunt's house and Connie said no, she wasn't interested, rolling her eyes to let mother know just what she thought of it. "Stay home alone then," her mother said sharply. Connie sat out back in a lawn chair and watched them drive away, her father quiet and bald, hunched around so that he could back the car out, her mother with a look that was still angry and not at all softened through the windshield, and in the back seat poor old June all dressed up as if she didn't know what a barbecue was, with all the running yelling kids and the flies. Connie sat with her eyes closed in the sun, dreaming and dazed with the warmth about her as if this were a kind of love, the caresses of love, and her mind slipped over onto thoughts of the boy she had been with the night before and how nice he had been, how sweet it always was, not the way someone like June would suppose but sweet, gentle, the way it was in movies and promised in songs; and when she opened her eyes she hardly knew where she was, the back yard ran off into weeds and a fence-line of trees and behind it the sky was perfectly blue and still. The asbestos "ranch house" that was now three years old startled her — it looked small. She shook her head as if to get awake.

It was too hot. She went inside the house and turned on the radio to drown out the quiet. She sat on the edge of her bed, barefoot, and listened for an hour and a half to a program called XYZ Sunday Jamboree, record after record of hard, fast, shrieking songs she sang along with, interspersed by exclamations from "Bobby King": "An' look here you girls at Napoleon's — Son and Charley want you to pay real close attention to this song coming up!"

And Connie paid close attention herself, bathed in a glow of slow-pulsed joy that seemed to rise mysteriously out of the music itself and lay languidly about the airless little room, breathed in and breathed out with each gentle rise and fall of her chest.

After a while she heard a car coming up the drive. She sat

up at once, startled, because it couldn't be her father so soon. The gravel kept crunching all the way in from the road — the driveway was long — and Connie ran to the window. It was a car she didn't know. It was an open jalopy, painted a bright gold that caught the sunlight opaquely. Her heart began to pound and her fingers snatched at her hair, checking it, and she whispered "Christ. Christ," wondering how bad she looked. The car came to a stop at the side door and the horn sounded four short taps as if this were a signal Connie knew.

She went into the kitchen and approached the door slowly, then hung out the screen door, her bare toes curling down off the step. There were two boys in the car and now she recognized the driver: he had shaggy, shabby black hair that looked crazy as a wig and he was grinning at her.

"I ain't late, am I?" he said.

"Who the hell do you think you are?" Connie said.

"Toldja I'd be out, didn't I?"

"I don't even know who you are."

She spoke sullenly, careful to show no interest or pleasure, and he spoke in a fast bright monotone. Connie looked past him to the other boy, taking her time. He had fair brown hair, with a lock that fell onto his forehead. His sideburns gave him a fierce, embarrassed look, but so far he hadn't even bothered to glance at her. Both boys wore sunglasses. The driver's glasses were metallic and mirrored everything in miniature.

"You wanta come for a ride?" he said.

Connie smirked and let her hair fall loose over one shoulder.

"Don'tcha like my car? New paint job," he said. "Hey."

"What?"

"You're cute."

She pretended to fidget, chasing flies away from the door. "Don'tcha believe me, or what?" he said.

"Look, I don't even know who you are," Connie said in disgust.

"Hey, Ellie's got a radio, see. Mine's broke down." He lifted his friend's arm and showed her the little transistor the boy was holding, and now Connie began to hear the music. It was the same program that was playing inside the house.

"Bobby King?" she said.

"I listen to him all the time. I think he's great."

"He's kind of great," Connie said reluctantly.

"Listen that guy's *great*. He knows where the action is."

Connie blushed a little, because the glasses made it impossible for her to see just what this boy was looking at. She couldn't decide if she liked him or if he was just a jerk, and so she dawdled in the doorway and wouldn't come down or go back inside. She said, "What's all that stuff painted on your car?"

"Can'tcha read it?" He opened the door very carefully, as if he was afraid it might fall off. He slid out just as carefully, planting his feet firmly on the ground, the tiny metallic world in his glasses slowing down like gelatine hardening and in the midst of it Connie's bright green blouse. "This here is my name, to begin with," he said. ARNOLD FRIEND was written in tarlike black letters on the side, with a drawing of a round grinning face that reminded Connie of a pumpkin, except it wore sunglasses. "I wanta introduce myself, I'm Arnold Friend and that's my real name and I'm gonna be your friend, honey, and inside the car's Ellie Oscar, he's kinda shy." Ellie brought his transistor radio up to his shoulder and balanced it there. "Now these numbers are a secret code, honey," Arnold Friend explained. He read off the numbers 33, 19, 17 and raised his eyebrows at her to see what she

thought of that, but she didn't think much of it. The left rear
fender had been smashed and around it was written on the
gleaming gold background: DONE BY CRAZY WOMAN
DRIVER. Connie had to laugh at that. Arnold Friend was
pleased at her laughter and looked up at her. "Around the
other side's a lot more — you wanta come and see them?"

"No."

"Why not?"

"Why should I?"

"Don'tcha wanta see what's on the car? Don'tcha wanta go
for a ride?"

"I don't know."

"Why not?"

"I got things to do."

"Like what?"

"Things."

He laughed as if she had said something funny. He slapped
his thighs. He was standing in a strange way, leaning back
against the car as if he were balancing himself. He wasn't
tall, only an inch or so taller than she would be if she came
down to him. Connie liked the way he was dressed, which
was the way all of them dressed: tight faded jeans stuffed into
black, scuffed boots, a belt that pulled his waist in and showed
how lean he was, and a white pullover shirt that was a little
soiled and showed the hard small muscles of his arms and
shoulders. He looked as if he probably did hard work, lifting
and carrying things. Even his neck looked muscular. And his
face was a familiar face, somehow: the jaw and chin and
cheeks slightly darkened, because he hadn't shaved for a day
or two, and the nose long and hawklike, sniffing as if she
were a treat he was going to gobble up and it was all a joke.

"Connie, you ain't telling the truth. This is your day set
aside for a ride with me and you know it," he said, still

laughing. The way he straightened and recovered from his fit of laughing showed that it had been all fake.

"How do you know what my name is?" she said suspiciously.

"It's Connie."

"Maybe and maybe not."

"I know my Connie," he said, wagging his finger. Now she remembered him even better, back at the restaurant, and her cheeks warmed at the thought of how she sucked in her breath just at the moment she passed him — how she must have looked to him. And he had remembered her. "Ellie and I come out here especially for you," he said. "Ellie can sit in back. How about it?"

"Where?"

"Where what?"

"Where're we going?"

He looked at her. He took off the sunglasses and she saw how pale the skin around his eyes was, like holes that were not in shadow but instead in light. His eyes were like chips of broken glass that catch the light in an amiable way. He smiled. It was as if the idea of going for a ride somewhere, to some place, was a new idea to him.

"Just for a ride, Connie sweetheart."

"I never said my name was Connie," she said.

"But I know what it is. I know your name and all about you, lots of things," Arnold Friend said. He had not moved yet but stood still leaning back against the side of his jalopy. "I took a special interest in you, such a pretty girl, and found out all about you like I know your parents and sister are gone somewheres and I know where and how long they're going to be gone, and I know who you were with last night, and your best girlfriend's name is Betty. Right?"

He spoke in a simple lilting voice, exactly as if he were

reciting the words to a song. His smile assured her that everything was fine. In the car Ellie turned up the volume on his
radio and did not bother to look around at them.

"Ellie can sit in the back seat," Arnold Friend said. He
indicated his friend with a casual jerk of his chin, as if Ellie
did not count and she should not bother with him.

"How'd you find out all that stuff?" Connie said.

"Listen: Betty Schultz and Tony Fitch and Jimmy Pettinger
and Nancy Pettinger," he said, in a chant. "Raymond Stanley
and Bob Hutter —"

"Do you know all those kids?"

"I know everybody."

"Look, you're kidding. You're not from around here."

"Sure."

"But — how come we never saw you before?"

"Sure you saw me before," he said. He looked down at
his boots, as if he were a little offended. "You just don't
remember."

"I guess I'd remember you," Connie said.

"Yeah?" He looked up at this, beaming. He was pleased.
He began to mark time with the music from Ellie's radio,
tapping his fists lightly together. Connie looked away from
his smile to the car, which was painted so bright it almost
hurt her eyes to look at it. She looked at that name,
ARNOLD FRIEND. And up at the front fender was
an expression that was familiar — MAN THE FLYING
SAUCERS. It was an expression kids had used the year before, but didn't use this year. She looked at it for a while as
if the words meant something to her that she did not yet
know.

"What're you thinking about? Huh?" Arnold Friend de-
manded. "Not worried about your hair blowing around in the
car, are you?"

"No."

"Think I maybe can't drive good?"

"How do I know?"

"You're a hard girl to handle. How come?" he said. "Don't you know I'm your friend? Didn't you see me put my sign in the air when you walked by?"

"What sign?"

"My sign." And he drew an X in the air, leaning out toward her. They were maybe ten feet apart. After his hand fell back to his side the X was still in the air, almost visible. Connie let the screen door close and stood perfectly still inside it, listening to the music from her radio and the boy's blend together. She stared at Arnold Friend. He stood there so stiffly relaxed, pretending to be relaxed, with one hand idly on the door handle as if he were keeping himself up that way and had no intention of ever moving again. She recognized most things about him, the tight jeans that showed his thighs and buttocks and the greasy leather boots and the tight shirt, and even that slippery friendly smile of his, that sleepy dreamy smile that all the boys used to get across ideas they didn't want to put into words. She recognized all this and also the singsong way he talked, slightly mocking, kidding, but serious and a little melancholy, and she recognized the way he tapped one fist against the other in homage to the perpetual music behind him. But all these things did not come together.

She said suddenly, "Hey, how old are you?"

His smile faded. She could see then that he wasn't a kid, he was much older — thirty, maybe more. At this knowledge her heart began to pound faster.

"That's a crazy thing to ask. Can'tcha see I'm your own age?"

"Like hell you are."

"Or maybe a coupla years older, I'm eighteen."

"Eighteen?" she said doubtfully.

He grinned to reassure her and lines appeared at the corners of his mouth. His teeth were big and white. He grinned so broadly his eyes became slits and she saw how thick the lashes were, thick and black as if painted with a black tarlike material. Then he seemed to become embarrassed, abruptly, and looked over his shoulder at Ellie. "Him, he's crazy," he said. "Ain't he a riot, he's a nut, a real character." Ellie was still listening to the music. His sunglasses told nothing about what he was thinking. He wore a bright orange shirt unbuttoned halfway to show his chest, which was a pale, bluish chest and not muscular like Arnold Friend's. His shirt collar was turned up all around and the very tips of the collar pointed out past his chin as if they were protecting him. He was pressing the transitor radio up against his ear and sat there in a kind of daze, right in the sun.

"He's kinda strange," Connie said.

"Hey, she says you're kinda strange! Kinda strange!" Arnold Friend cried. He pounded on the car to get Ellie's attention. Ellie turned for the first time and Connie saw with shock that he wasn't a kid either — he had a fair, hairless face, cheeks reddened slightly as if the veins grew too close to the surface of his skin, the face of a forty-year-old baby. Connie felt a wave of dizziness rise in her at this sight and she stared at him as if waiting for something to change the shock of the moment, make it all right again. Ellie's lips kept shaping words, mumbling along with the words blasting in his ear.

"Maybe you two better go away," Connie said faintly.

"What? How come?" Arnold Friend cried. "We come out here to take you for a ride. It's Sunday." He had the voice of the man on the radio now. It was the same voice, Connie thought. "Don'tcha know it's Sunday all day and honey, no matter who you were with last night today you're with Arnold Friend and don't you forget it! — Maybe you better step out here," he said, and this last was in a different voice. It was a little flatter, as if the heat was finally getting to him.

"No. I got things to do."

"Hey."

"You two better leave."

"We ain't leaving until you come with us."

"Like hell I am —"

"Connie, don't fool around with me. I mean, I mean, don't fool *around,*" he said, shaking his head. He laughed incredulously. He placed his sunglasses on top of his head, carefully, as if he were indeed wearing a wig, and brought the stems down behind his ears. Connie stared at him, another wave of dizziness and fear rising in her so that for a moment he wasn't even in focus but was just a blur, standing there against his gold car, and she had the idea that he had driven up the driveway all right but had come from nowhere before that and belonged nowhere and that everything about him and even about the music that was so familiar to her was only half real.

"If my father comes and sees you —"

"He ain't coming. He's at a barbecue."

"How do you know that?"

"Aunt Tillie's. Right now they're — uh — they're drinking. Sitting around," he said vaguely, squinting as if he were staring all the way to town and over to Aunt Tillie's back yard. Then the vision seemed to get clear and he nodded energetically. "Yeah. Sitting around. There's your sister in a blue dress, huh? And high heels, the poor sad bitch — nothing like you, sweetheart! And your mother's helping some fat woman with the corn, they're cleaning the corn — husking the corn —"

"What fat woman?" Connie cried.

"How do I know what fat woman, I don't know every goddam fat woman in the world!" Arnold laughed.

"Oh, that's Mrs. Hornby . . . Who invited her?" Connie said. She felt a little light-headed. Her breath was coming quickly.

"She's too fat. I don't like them fat. I like them the way you are, honey," he said, smiling sleepily at her. They stared at each other for a while, through the screen door. He said softly, "Now what you're going to do is this: you're going to come out that door. You're going to sit up front with me and Ellie's going to sit in the back, the hell with Ellie, right? This isn't Ellie's date. You're my date. I'm your lover, honey."

"What? You're crazy —"

"Yes, I'm your lover. You don't know what that is but you will," he said. "I know that too. I know all about you. But look: it's real nice and you couldn't ask for nobody better than me, or more polite. I always keep my word. I'll tell you how it is, I'm always nice at first, the first time. I'll hold you so tight you won't think you have to try to get away or pretend anything because you'll know you can't. And I'll come inside you where it's all secret and you'll give in to me and you'll love me —"

"Shut up! You're crazy!" Connie said. She backed away from the door. She put her hands against her ears as if she'd heard something terrible, something not meant for her. "People don't talk like that, you're crazy," she muttered. Her heart was almost too big now for her chest and its pumping made sweat break out all over her. She looked out to see Arnold Friend pause and then take a step toward the porch lurching. He almost fell. But, like a clever drunken man, he managed to catch his balance. He wobbled in his high boots and grabbed hold of one of the porch posts.

"Honey?" he said. "You still listening?"

"Get the hell out of here!"

"Be nice, honey. Listen."

"I'm going to call the police —"

He wobbled again and out of the side of his mouth came a fast spat curse, an aside not meant for her to hear. But even this "Christ!" sounded forced. Then he began to smile again. She watched this smile come, awkward as if he were smiling from inside a mask. His whole face as a mask, she thought wildly, tanned down onto his throat but then running out as if he had plastered makeup on his face but had forgotten about his throat.

"Honey —? Listen, here's how it is. I always tell the truth and I promise you this: I ain't coming in that house after you."

"You better not! I'm going to call the police if you — if you don't —"

"Honey," he said, talking right through her voice, "honey, I'm not coming in there but you are coming out here. You know why?"

She was panting. The kitchen looked like a place she had never seen before, some room she had run inside but which wasn't good enough, wasn't going to help her. The kitchen window had never had a curtain, after three years, and there were dishes in the sink for her to do — probably — and if you ran your hand across the table you'd probably feel something sticky there.

"You listening, honey? Hey?"

"— going to call the police —"

"Soon as you touch the phone I don't need to keep my promise and can come inside. You won't want that."

She rushed forward and tried to lock the door. Her fingers were shaking. "But why lock it," Arnold Friend said gently, talking right into her face. "It's just a screen door. It's just nothing." One of his boots was at a strange angle, as if his foot wasn't in it. It pointed out to the left, bent at the ankle. "I mean, anybody can break through a screen door and glass and wood and iron or anything else if he needs to, anybody at all and specially Arnold Friend. If the place got lit up with a fire honey you'd come runnin' out into my arms, right into my arms an' safe at home — like you knew I was your lover and'd stopped fooling around. I don't mind a nice shy girl but I don't like no fooling around." Part of those words were spoken with a slight rhythmic lilt, and Connie somehow recognized them — the echo of a song from last year, about a girl rushing into her boyfriend's arms and coming home again —

Connie stood barefoot on the linoleum floor, staring at him. "What do you want?" she whispered.

"I want you," he said.

"What?"

"Seen you that night and thought, that's the one, yes sir. I never needed to look any more."

"But my father's coming back. He's coming to get me. I had to wash my hair first —" She spoke in a dry, rapid voice, hardly raising it for him to hear.

"No, your daddy is not coming and yes, you had to wash your hair and you washed it for me. It's nice and shining and all for me, I thank you, sweetheart," he said, with a mock bow, but again he almost lost his balance. He had to bend and adjust his boots. Evidently his feet did not go all the way down; the boots must have been stuffed with something so that he would seem taller. Connie stared out at him and behind him Ellie in the car, who seemed to be looking off toward Connie's right, into nothing. This Ellie said, pulling the words out of the air one after another as if he were just discovering them, "You want me to pull out the phone?"

"Shut your mouth and keep it shut," Arnold Friend said, his face red from bending over or maybe from embarrassment because Connie had seen his boots. "This ain't none of your business."

"What — what are you doing? What do you want?" Connie said. "If I call the police they'll get you, they'll arrest you —"

"Promise was not to come in unless you touch that phone, and I'll keep that promise," he said. He resumed his erect position and tried to force his shoulders back. He sounded like a hero in a movie, declaring something important. He spoke too loudly and it was as if he were speaking to someone behind Connie. "I ain't made plans for coming in that house where I don't belong but just for you to come out to me, the way you should. Don't you know who I am?"

"You're crazy," she whispered. She backed away from the door but did not want to go into another part of the house, as if this would give him permission to come through the door. "What do you . . . You're crazy, you . . ."

"Huh? "What're you saying, honey?"

Her eyes darted everywhere in the kitchen. She could not remember what it was, this room.

"This is how it is, honey: you come out and we'll drive away, have a nice ride. But if you don't come out we're gonna wait till your people come home and then they're all going to get it."

"You want that telephone pulled out?" Ellie said. He held the radio away from his ear and grimaced, as if without the radio the air was too much for him.

"I toldja shut up, Ellie," Arnold Friend said, "you're deaf, get a hearing aid, right? Fix yourself up. This little girl's no trouble and's gonna be nice to me, so Ellie keep to yourself, this ain't your date — right? Don't hem in on me. Don't hog. Don't crush. Don't bird dog. Don't trail me," he said in a rapid meaningless voice, as if he were running through all the expressions he'd learned but was no longer sure which one of them was in style, then rushing on to new ones, making them up with his eyes closed, "Don't crawl under my fence, don't squeeze in my chipmunk hole, don't sniff my glue, suck my popsicle, keep your own greasy fingers on yourself!" He shaded his eyes and peered in at Connie, who was backed against the kitchen table. "Don't mind him honey he's just a creep. He's a dope. Right? I'm the boy for you and like I said you come out here nice like a lady and give me your hand, and nobody else gets hurt, I mean, your nice old bald-headed daddy and your mummy and your sister in her high heels. Because listen: why bring them in this?"

"Leave me alone," Connie whispered.

"Hey, you know that old woman down the road, the one with the chickens and stuff — you know her?"

"She's dead!"

"Dead? What? You know her?" Arnold Friend said.

"She's dead —"

"Don't you like her?"

"She's dead — she's — she isn't here anymore —"

"But don't you like her, I mean, you got something against her? Some grudge or something?" Then his voice dipped as if he were conscious of a rudeness. He touched the sunglasses perched on top of his head as if to make sure they were still there. "Now you be a good girl."

"What are you going to do?"

"Just two things, or maybe three," Arnold Friend said. "But I promise it won't last long and you'll like me the way you get to like people you're close to. You will. It's all over for you here, so come on out. You don't want your people in any trouble, do you?"

She turned and bumped against a chair or something, hurting her leg, but she ran into the back room and picked up the telephone. Something roared in her ear, a tiny roaring, and she was so sick with fear that she could do nothing but listen to it — the telephone was clammy and very heavy and her fingers groped down to the dial but were too weak to touch it. She began to scream into the phone, into the roaring. She cried out, she cried for her mother, she felt her breath start jerking back and forth in her lungs as if it were something Arnold Friend were stabbing her with again and again with no tenderness. A noisy sorrowful wailing rose all about her and she was locked inside it the way she was locked inside this house.

After a while she could hear again. She was sitting on the floor with her wet back against the wall.

Arnold Friend was saying from the door, "That's a good girl. Put the phone back."

She kicked the phone away from her.

"No, honey. Pick it up. Put it back right."

She picked it up and put it back. The dial tone stopped.

"That's a good girl. Now you come outside."

She was hollow with what had been fear, but what was now just an emptiness. All that screaming had blasted it out of her. She sat, one leg cramped under her, and deep inside her brain was something like a pinpoint of light that kept going and would not let her relax. She thought, I'm not going to see my mother again. She thought, I'm not going to sleep in my bed again. Her bright green blouse was all wet.

Arnold Friend said, in a gentle-loud voice that was like a stage voice, "The place where you came from ain't there anymore, and where you had in mind to go is canceled out. This place you are now — inside your daddy's house — is nothing but a cardboard box I can knock down anytime. You know that and always did know it. You hear me?"

She thought, I have got to think. I have to know what to do.

"We'll go out to a nice field, out in the country here where it smells so nice and it's sunny," Arnold Friend said. "I'll have my arms tight around you so you won't need to try to get away and I'll show you what love is like, what it does. The hell with this house! It looks solid all right," he said. He ran a fingernail down the screen and the noise did not make Connie shiver, as it would have the day before. "Now put your hand on your heart, honey. Feel that? That feels solid too but we know better, be nice to me, be sweet like you can because what else is there for a girl like you but to be sweet and pretty and give in? — and get away before her people come back?"

She felt her pounding heart. Her hand seemed to enclose it. She thought for the first time in her life that it was nothing that was hers, that belonged to her, but just a pounding, living thing inside this body that wasn't really hers either.

"You don't want them to get hurt," Arnold Friend went on. "Now get up, honey. Get up all by yourself."

She stood.

"Now turn this way. That's right. Come over here to me — Ellie, put that away, didn't I tell you? You dope. You miserable creepy dope," Arnold Friend said. His words were not angry but only part of an incantation. The incantation was kindly. "Now come out through the kitchen to me honey and let's see a smile, try it, you're a brave sweet little girl and now they're eating corn and hot dogs cooked to bursting over an outdoor fire, and they don't know one thing about you and never did and honey you're better than them because not a one of them would have done this for you."

Connie felt the linoleum under her feet; it was cool. She brushed her hair back out of her eyes. Arnold Friend let go of the post tentatively and opened his arms for her, his elbows pointing in toward each other and his wrists limp, to show that this was an embarrassed embrace and a little mocking, he didn't want to make her self-conscious.

She put out her hand against the screen. She watched herself push the door slowly open as if she were safe back somewhere in the other doorway, watching this body and this head of long hair moving out into the sunlight where Arnold Friend waited.

"My sweet little blue-eyed girl," he said, in a half-sung sigh that had nothing to do with her brown eyes but was taken up just the same by the vast sunlit reaches of the land behind him and on all sides of him, so much land that Connie had never seen before and did not recognize except to know that she was going to it.

American History

Judith Ortiz-Cofer

I once read in a "Ripley's Believe It or Not" column that Paterson, New Jersey, is the place where the Straight and Narrow (streets) intersect. The Puerto Rican tenement known as *El Building* was one block up from Straight. It was, in fact, the corner of Straight and Market; not "at" the corner, but *the* corner. At almost any hour of the day, El Building was like a monstrous jukebox, blasting out *salsas* from open windows as the residents, mostly new immigrants just up from the island, tried to drown out whatever they were currently enduring with loud music. But the day President Kennedy was shot there was a profound silence in El Building; even the abusive tongues of viragoes, the cursing of the unemployed, and the screeching of small children had been somehow muted. President Kennedy was a saint to these people. In fact, soon his photograph would be hung alongside the Sacred Heart and over the spiritist altars that many women kept in their apartments. He would become part of the hierarchy of martyrs they prayed to for favors that only one who had died for a cause would understand.

On the day that President Kennedy was shot, my ninth

grade class had been out in the fenced playground of Public School Number 13. We had been given "free" exercise time and had been ordered by our P.E. teacher, Mr. DePalma, to "keep moving." That meant that the girls should jump rope and the boys toss basketballs through a hoop at the far end of the yard. He in the meantime would "keep an eye" on us from just inside the building.

It was a cold gray day in Paterson. The kind that warns of early snow. I was miserable, since I had forgotten my gloves, and my knuckles were turning red and raw from the jump rope. I was also taking a lot of abuse from the black girls for not turning the rope hard and fast enough for them.

"Hey, Skinny Bones, pump it, girl. Ain't you got no energy today?" Gail, the biggest of the black girls had the other end of the rope, yelled, "Didn't you eat your rice and beans and pork chops for breakfast today?"

The other girls picked up the "pork chop" and made it into a refrain: "pork chop, pork chop, did you eat your pork chop?" They entered the double ropes in pairs and exited without tripping or missing a beat. I felt a burning on my cheeks and then my glasses fogged up so that I could not manage to coordinate the jump rope with Gail. The chill was doing to me what it always did; entering my bones, making me cry, humiliating me. I hated the city, especially in winter. I hated Public School Number 13. I hated my skinny flatchested body, and I envied the black girls who could jump rope so fast that their legs became a blur. They always seemed to be warm while I froze.

There was only one source of beauty and light for me that school year. The only thing I had anticipated at the start of the semester. That was seeing Eugene. In August, Eugene and his family had moved into the only house on the block that had a yard and trees. I could see his place from my

window in El Building. In fact, if I sat on the fire escape I
was literally suspended above Eugene's backyard. It was my
favorite spot to read my library books in the summer. Until
that August the house had been occupied by an old Jewish
couple. Over the years I had become part of their family,
without their knowing it, of course. I had a view of their
kitchen and their backyard, and though I could not hear what
they said, I knew when they were arguing, when one of them
was sick, and many other things. I knew all this by watching
them at mealtimes. I could see their kitchen table, the sink,
and the stove. During good times, he sat at the table and
read his newspapers while she fixed the meals. If they argued,
he would leave and the old woman would sit and stare at
nothing for a long time. When one of them was sick, the
other would come and get things from the kitchen and carry
them out on a tray. The old man had died in June. The last
week of school I had not seen him at the table at all. Then
one day I saw that there was a crowd in the kitchen. The old
woman had finally emerged from the house on the arm of a
stocky middle-aged woman, whom I had seen there a few
times before, maybe her daughter. Then a man had carried
out suitcases. The house had stood empty for weeks. I had
had to resist the temptation to climb down into the yard and
water the flowers the old lady had taken such good care of.

By the time Eugene's family moved in, the yard was a
tangled mass of weeds. The father had spent several days
mowing, and when he finished, from where I sat, I didn't see
the red, yellow, and purple clusters that meant flowers to me.
I didn't see this family sit down at the kitchen table together.
It was just the mother, a red-headed tall woman who wore a
white uniform — a nurse's, I guessed it was; the father was
gone before I got up in the morning and was never there at
dinnertime. I only saw him on weekends when they some-

times sat on lawn chairs under the oak tree, each hidden behind a section of the newspaper; and there was Eugene. He was tall and blond, and he wore glasses. I liked him right away because he sat at the kitchen table and read books for hours. That summer, before we had even spoken one word to each other, I kept him company on my fire escape.

Once school started I looked for him in all my classes, but P.S. 13 was a huge, overpopulated place and it took me days and many discreet questions to discover that Eugene was in honors classes for all his subjects, classes that were not open to me because English was not my first language, though I was a straight A student. After much maneuvering I managed to "run into him" in the hallway where his locker was — on the other side of the building from mine — and in study hall at the library, where he first seemed to notice me, but did not speak; and finally, on the way home after school one day when I decided to approach him directly, though my stomach was doing somersaults.

I was ready for rejection, snobbery, the worst. But when I came up to him, practically panting in my nervousness, and blurted out: "You're Eugene. Right?" He smiled, pushed his glasses up on his nose, and nodded. I saw then that he was blushing deeply. Eugene liked me, but he was shy. I did most of the talking that day. He nodded and smiled a lot. In the weeks that followed, we walked home together. He would linger at the corner of El Building for a few minutes then walk down to his two-story house. It was not until Eugene moved into that house that I noticed that El Building blocked most of the sun, and that the only spot that got a little sunlight during the day was the tiny square of earth the old woman had planted with flowers.

I did not tell Eugene that I could see inside his kitchen from my bedroom. I felt dishonest, but I liked my secret sharing of his evenings, especially now that I knew what he was reading since we chose our books together at the school library.

One day my mother came into my room as I was sitting on the windowsill staring out. In her abrupt way she said, "Elena, you are acting moony." *Enamorada* was what she really said, that is — like a girl stupidly infatuated. Since I had turned fourteen and started menstruating my mother had been more vigilant than ever. She acted as if I was going to go crazy or explode or something if she didn't watch me and nag me all the time about being a *señorita* now. She kept talking about virtue, morality, and other subjects that did not interest me in the least. My mother was unhappy in Paterson, but my father had a good job at the bluejeans factory in Passaic and soon, he kept assuring us, we would be moving to our own house there. Every Sunday we drove out to the suburbs of Paterson, Clifton, and Passaic, out to where people mowed grass on Sundays in the summer, and where children made snowmen in the winter from pure white snow, not like the gray slush of Paterson, which seemed to fall from the sky in that hue. I had learned to listen to my parents' dreams, which were spoken in Spanish, as fairy tales, like the stories about life in the island paradise of Puerto Rico before I was born. I had been to the island once as a little girl, to grandmother's funeral, and all I remembered was wailing women in black, my mother becoming hysterical and being given a pill that made her sleep two days, and me feeling lost in a crowd of strangers all claiming to be my aunts, uncles, and cousins. I had actually been glad to return to the city. We had not been back there since then, though my parents talked constantly about buying a house on the beach someday, retiring on the island — that was a common topic among the residents of El

Building. As for me, I was going to go to college and become a teacher.

But after meeting Eugene I began to think of the present more than of the future. What I wanted now was to enter that house I had watched for so many years. I wanted to see the other rooms where the old people had lived, and where the boy spent his time. Most of all, I wanted to sit at the kitchen table with Eugene like two adults, like the old man and his wife had done, maybe drink some coffee and talk about books. I had started reading *Gone With the Wind.* I was enthralled by it, with the daring and the passion of the beautiful girl living in a mansion, and with her devoted parents and the slaves who did everything for them. I didn't believe such a world had ever really existed, and I wanted to ask Eugene some questions since he and his parents, he had told me, had come up from Georgia, the same place where the novel was set. His father worked for a company that had transferred him to Paterson. His mother was very unhappy, Eugene said, in his beautiful voice that rose and fell over words in a strange, lilting way. The kids at school called him "the hick" and made fun of the way he talked. I knew I was his only friend so far, and I liked that, though I felt sad for him sometimes. "Skinny Bones" and the "Hick" was what they called us at school when we were seen together.

The day Mr. DePalma came out into the cold and asked us to line up in front of him was the day that President Kennedy was shot. Mr. DePalma, a short, muscular man with slicked-down black hair, was the science teacher, P.E. coach, and disciplinarian at P.S. 13. He was the teacher to whose homeroom you got assigned if you were a troublemaker, and the man called out to break up playground fights, and to escort violently angry teen-agers to the office. And Mr. De-

Palma was the man who called your parents in for "a conference."

That day, he stood in front of two rows of mostly black
and Puerto Rican kids, brittle from their efforts to "keep moving" on a November day that was turning bitter cold. Mr.
DePalma, to our complete shock, was crying. Not just silent
adult tears, but really sobbing. There were a few titters from
the back of the line where I stood shivering.

"Listen." Mr. DePalma raised his arms over his head as if
he were about to conduct an orchestra. His voice broke, and
he covered his face with his hands. His barrel chest was heav-
ing. Someone giggled behind me.

"Listen," he repeated, "something awful has happened." A
strange gurgling came from his throat, and he turned around
and spat on the cement behind him.

"Gross," someone said, and there was a lot of laughter.

"The President is dead, you idiots. I should have known
that wouldn't mean anything to a bunch of losers like you
kids. Go home." He was shrieking now. No one moved for
a minute or two, but then a big girl let out a "Yeah!" and
ran to get her books piled up with the others against the brick
wall of the school building. The others followed in a mad
scramble to get to their things before somebody caught on. It
was still an hour to the dismissal bell.

A little scared, I headed for El Building. There was an
eerie feeling on the streets. I looked into Mario's drugstore, a
favorite hangout for the high school crowd, but there were
only a couple of old Jewish men at the soda-bar talking with
the short order cook in tones that sounded almost angry, but
they were keeping their voices low. Even the traffic on one
of the busiest intersections in Paterson — Straight Street and
Park Avenue — seemed to be moving slower. There were no
horns blasting that day. At El Building, the usual little group

of unemployed men were not hanging out on the front stoop making it difficult for women to enter the front door. No music spilled out from open doors in the hallway. When I walked into our apartment, I found my mother sitting in front of the grainy picture of the television set.

She looked up at me with a tear-streaked face and just said, "*Dios mío*," turning back to the set as if it were pulling at her eyes. I went into my room.

Though I wanted to feel the right thing about President Kennedy's death, I could not fight the feeling of elation that stirred in my chest. Today was the day I was to visit Eugene in his house. He had asked me to come over after school to study for an American History test with him. We had also planned to walk to the public library together. I looked down into his yard. The oak tree was bare of leaves and the ground looked gray with ice. The light through the large kitchen window of his house told me that El Building blocked the sun to such an extent that they had to turn lights on in the middle of the day. I felt ashamed about it. But the white kitchen table with the lamp hanging just above it looked cozy and inviting. I would soon sit there, across from Eugene, and I would tell him about my perch just above his house. Maybe I should.

In the next thirty minutes I changed clothes, put on a little pink lipstick, and got my books together. Then I went in to tell my mother that I was going to a friend's house to study. I did not expect her reaction.

"You are going out *today?*" The way she said "today" sounded as if a storm warning had been issued. It was said in utter disbelief. Before I could answer, she came toward me and held my elbows as I clutched my books.

"*Hija*, the President has been killed. We must show respect. He was a great man. Come to church with me tonight."

She tried to embrace me, but my books were in the way. My first impulse was to comfort her, she seemed so distraught, but I had to meet Eugene in fifteen minutes.

"I have a test to study for, Mama. I will be home by eight."

"You are forgetting who you are, *niña*. I have seen you staring down at that boy's house. You are heading for humiliation and pain." My mother said this in Spanish and in a resigned tone that surprised me, as if she had no intention of stopping me from "heading for humiliation and pain." I started for the door. She sat in front of the TV holding a white handkerchief to her face.

I walked out to the street and around the chain-link fence that separated El Building from Eugene's house. The yard was neatly edged around the little walk that led to the door. It always amazed me how Paterson, the inner core of the city, had no apparent logic to its architecture. Small, neat, single residences like this one could be found right next to huge, dilapidated apartment buildings like El Building. My guess was that the little houses had been there first, then the immigrants had come in droves, and the monstrosities had been raised for them — the Italians, the Irish, the Jews, and now us, the Puerto Ricans and the blacks. The door was painted a deep green: *verde,* the color of hope. I had heard my mother say it: *Verde — Esperanza.*

I knocked softly. A few suspenseful moments later, the door opened just a crack. The red, swollen face of a woman appeared. She had a halo of red hair floating over a delicate ivory face — the face of a doll — with freckles on the nose. Her smudged eye make-up made her look unreal to me, like a mannequin seen through a warped store window.

"What do you want?" Her voice was tiny and sweet-sounding, like a little girl's, but her tone was not friendly.

"I'm Eugene's friend. He asked me over. To study." I thrust

out my books, a silly gesture that embarrassed me almost
immediately.

"You live there?" She pointed up to El Building, which
looked particularly ugly, like a gray prison with its many dirty
windows and rusty fire escapes. The woman had stepped halfway out and I could see that she wore a white nurse's uniform
with St. Joseph's Hospital on the name tag.

"Yes. I do."

She looked intently at me for a couple of heartbeats, then
said as if to herself, "I don't know how you people do it."
Then directly to me: "Listen. Honey. Eugene doesn't want
to study with you. He is a smart boy. Doesn't need help. You
understand me. I am truly sorry if he told you you could come
over. He cannot study with you. It's nothing personal. You
understand? We won't be in this place much longer, no need
for him to get close to people — it'll just make it harder for
him later. Run back home now."

I couldn't move. I just stood there in shock at hearing these
things said to me in such a honey-drenched voice. I had never
heard an accent like hers, except for Eugene's softer version.
It was as if she were singing me a little song.

"What's wrong? Didn't you hear what I said?" She seemed
very angry, and I finally snapped out of my trance. I turned
away from the green door, and heard her close it gently.

Our apartment was empty when I got home. My mother
was in someone else's kitchen, seeking the solace she needed.
Father would come in from his late shift at midnight. I would
hear them talking softly in the kitchen for hours that night.
They would not discuss their dreams for the future, or life in
Puerto Rico, as they often did; that night they would talk
sadly about the young widow and her two children, as if they
were family. For the next few days, we would observe *luto* in
our apartment; that is, we would practice restraint and si-

lence — no loud music or laughter. Some of the women of El Building would wear black for weeks.

That night, I lay in my bed trying to feel the right thing for our dead president. But the tears that came up from a deep source inside me were strictly for me. When my mother came to the door, I pretended to be sleeping. Sometime during the night, I saw from my bed the streetlight come on. It had a pink halo around it. I went to my window and pressed my face to the cool glass. Looking up at the light, I could see the white snow falling like a lace veil over its face. I did not look down to see it turning gray as it touched the ground below.

Raymond's Run

Toni Cade Bambara

I don't have much work to do around the house like some girls. My mother does that. And I don't have to earn my pocket money by hustling; George runs errands for the big boys and sells Christmas cards. And anything else that's got to get done, my father does. All I have to do in life is mind my brother Raymond, which is enough.

Sometimes I slip and say my little brother Raymond. But as any fool can see he's much bigger and he's older too. But a lot of people call him my little brother 'cause he needs looking after 'cause he's not quite right. And a lot of smart mouths got lots to say about that too, especially when George was minding him. But now, if anybody has anything to say to Raymond, anything to say about his big head, they have to come by me. And I don't play the dozens or believe in standing around with somebody in my face doing a lot of talking. I much rather just knock you down and take my chances, even if I am a little girl with skinny arms and a squeaky voice, which is how I got the name Squeaky. And if things get too rough, I run. And as anybody can tell you, I'm the fastest thing on two feet.

There is no track meet that I don't win the first place medal. I used to win the twenty-yard dash when I was a little kid in kindergarten. Nowadays, it's the fifty-yard dash. And tomorrow I'm subject to run the quarter-meter relay all by myself and come in first, second, and third. The big kids call me Mercury 'cause I'm the swiftest thing in the neighborhood. Everybody knows that — except two people who know better, my father and me. He can beat me to Amsterdam Avenue with me having a two fire-hydrant head start and him running with his hands in his pockets and whistling. But that's private information. 'Cause can you imagine some thirty-five-year-old man stuffing himself into PAL shorts to race little kids? So as far as everyone's concerned, I'm the fastest and that goes for Gretchen too, who has put out the tale that she is going to win the first-place medal this year. Ridiculous. In the second place, she's got short legs. In the third place, she's got freckles. In the first place, no one can beat me and that's all there is to it.

I'm standing on the corner admiring the weather and about to take a stroll down Broadway so I can practice my breathing exercises, and I've got Raymond walking on the inside close to the buildings, 'cause he's subject to fits of fantasy and starts thinking he's a circus performer and that the curb is a tightrope strung high in the air. And sometimes after a rain he likes to step down off his tightrope right into the gutter and slosh around, getting his shoes and cuffs wet. Then I get hit when I get home. Or sometimes if you don't watch him, he'll dash across traffic to the island in the middle of Broadway and give the pigeons a fit. Then I have to go behind him apologizing to all the old people sitting around trying to get some sun and getting all upset with the pigeons fluttering around them, scattering their newspapers and upsetting the waxpaper lunches in their laps. So I keep Raymond on the inside of me, and he plays like he's driving a stage coach, which is O.K. by me so long as he doesn't run me over or interrupt my breathing exercises, which I have to do on account of I'm serious about my running, and I don't care who knows it.

Now some people like to act like things come easy to them, won't let on that they practice. Not me. I'll high-prance down 34th Street like a rodeo pony to keep my knees strong even if it does get my mother uptight so that she walks ahead like she's not with me, don't know me, is all by herself on a shopping trip, and I am somebody else's crazy child. Now you take Cynthia Procter for instance. She's just the opposite. If there's a test tomorrow, she'll say something like, "Oh, I guess I'll play handball this afternoon and watch television tonight," just to let you know she ain't thinking about the test. Or like last week when she won the spelling bee for the millionth time: "A good thing you got *receive*, Squeaky, 'cause I would have got it wrong. I completely forgot about the spelling bee." And she'll clutch the lace on her blouse like it was a narrow escape. Oh, brother. But of course when I pass her house on my early morning trots around the block, she is practicing the scales on the piano over and over and over and over. Then in music class she always lets herself get bumped around so she falls accidentally on purpose onto the piano stool and is so surprised to find herself sitting there that she decides just for fun to try out the ole keys. And what do you know — Chopin's waltzes just spring out of her fingertips and she's the most surprised thing in the world. A regular prodigy. I could kill people like that. I stay up all night studying the words for the spelling bee. And you can see me any time of day practicing running. I never walk if I can trot, and shame on Raymond if he can't keep up. But of course he does, 'cause if he hangs back someone's liable to walk up to him and get smart, or take his allowance from him, or ask him where he got that great big pumpkin head. People are so stupid sometimes.

So I'm strolling down Broadway breathing out and breathing in on counts of seven, which is my lucky number, and here comes Gretchen and her sidekicks: Mary Louise, who used to be a friend of mine when she first moved to Harlem from Baltimore and got beat up by everybody till I took up for her on account of her mother and my mother used to sing in the same choir when they were young girls, but people ain't grateful, so now she hangs out with the new girl Gretchen and talks about me like a dog; and Rosie, who is as fat as I am skinny and has a big mouth where Raymond is concerned and is too stupid to know that there is not a big deal of difference between herself and Raymond and that she can't afford to throw stones. So they are steady coming up Broadway and I see right away that it's going to be one of those Dodge City scenes 'cause the street ain't that big and they're close to the buildings just as we are. First I think I'll step into the candy store and look over the new comics and let them pass. But that's chicken and I've got a reputation to consider. So then I think I'll just walk straight on through them or even over them if necessary. But as they get to me, they slow down. I'm ready to fight, 'cause like I said I don't feature a whole lot of chit-chat, I much prefer to just knock you down right from the jump and save everybody a lotta precious time.

"You signing up for the May Day races?" smiles Mary Louise, only it's not a smile at all. A dumb question like that doesn't deserve an answer. Besides, there's just me and Gretchen standing there really, so no use wasting my breath talking to shadows.

"I don't think you're going to win this time," says Rosie, trying to signify with her hands on her hips all salty, completely forgetting that I have whupped her behind many times for less salt than that.

"I always win 'cause I'm the best," I say straight at Gretchen, who is, as far as I'm concerned, the only one talking in this ventriloquist-dummy routine. Gretchen smiles, but it's not a smile, and I'm thinking that girls never really smile at each other because they don't know how and don't want to know how and there's probably no one to teach us how, 'cause grown-up girls don't know either. Then they all look at Raymond, who has just brought his mule team to a standstill. And they're about to see what trouble they can get into through him.

"What grade you in now, Raymond?"

"You got anything to say to my brother, you say it to me, Mary Louise Williams of Raggedy Town, Baltimore."

"What are you, his mother?" sasses Rosie.

"That's right, Fatso. And the next word out of anybody and I'll be *their* mother too." So they just stand there and Gretchen shifts from one leg to the other and so do they. Then Gretchen puts her hands on her hips and is about to say something with her freckle-face self but doesn't. Then she walks around me, looking me up and down, but keeps walking up Broadway, and her sidekicks follow her. So me and Raymond smile at each other and he says, "Giddyap" to his team and I continue with my breathing exercises, strolling down Broadway toward the ice man of 145th with not a care in the world 'cause I am Miss Quicksilver herself.

I take my time getting to the park on May Day because the track meet is the last thing on the program. The biggest thing on the program is the May Pole dancing, which I can do without, thank you, even if my mother thinks it's a shame I don't take part and act like a girl for a change. You'd think my mother'd be grateful not to have to make me a white organdy dress with a big satin sash and buy me new white baby-doll shoes that can't be taken out of the box till the big day. You'd think she'd be glad her daughter ain't out there prancing around a May Pole getting the new clothes all dirty and sweaty and trying to act like a fairy or a flower or whatever you're supposed to be when you should be trying to be yourself, whatever that is, which is, as far as I am concerned, a poor black girl who really can't afford to buy shoes and a new dress you only wear once a lifetime 'cause it won't fit next year.

I was once a strawberry in a Hansel and Gretel pageant when I was in nursery school and didn't have no better sense than to dance on tiptoe with my arms in a circle over my head doing umbrella steps and being a perfect fool just so my mother and father could come dressed up and clap. You'd think they'd know better than to encourage that kind of nonsense. I am not a strawberry. I do not dance on my toes. I run. That is what I am all about. So I always come late to the May Day program, just in time to get my number pinned on and lie in the grass till they announce the fifty-yard dash.

I put Raymond in the little swings, which is a tight squeeze this year and will be impossible next year. Then I look around for Mr. Pearson, who pins the numbers on. I'm really looking for Gretchen if you want to know the truth, but she's not around. The park is jam-packed. Parents in hats and corsages and breast-pocket handkerchiefs peeking up. Kids in white dresses and light-blue suits. The parkees unfolding chairs and chasing the rowdy kids from Lenox as if they had no right to be there. The big guys with their caps on backwards, leaning against the fence swirling the basketballs on the tips of their fingers, waiting for all these crazy people to clear out the park so they can play. Most of the kids in my class are carrying bass drums and glockenspiels and flutes. You'd think they'd put in a few bongos or something for real like that.

Then here comes Mr. Pearson with his clipboard and his cards and pencils and whistles and safety pins and fifty million other things he's always dropping all over the place with his clumsy self. He sticks out in a crowd because he's on stilts. We used to call him Jack and the Beanstalk to get him mad. But I'm the only one that can outrun him and get away, and I'm too grown for that silliness now.

"Well, Squeaky," he says, checking my name off the list and handing me number seven and two pins. And I'm thinking he's got no right to call me Squeaky, if I can't call him Beanstalk.

"Hazel Elizabeth Deborah Parker," I correct him and tell him to write it down on his board.

"Well, Hazel Elizabeth Deborah Parker, going to give someone else a break this year?" I squint at him real hard to see if he is seriously thinking I should lose the race on purpose just to give someone else a break. "Only six girls running this time," he continues, shaking his head sadly like it's my fault all of New York didn't turn out in sneakers. "That new girl should give you a run for your money." He looks around the park for Gretchen like a periscope in a submarine movie. "Wouldn't it be a nice gesture if you were . . . to ahhh . . ."

I give him such a look he couldn't finish putting that idea into words. Grown-ups got a lot of nerve sometimes. I pin number seven to myself and stomp away, I'm so burnt. And I go straight for the track and stretch out on the grass while the band winds up with "Oh, the Monkey Wrapped His Tail Around the Flag Pole," which my teacher calls by some other name. The man on the loudspeaker is calling everyone over to the track and I'm on my back looking at the sky, trying to pretend I'm in the country, but I can't, because even grass in the city feels hard as sidewalk, and there's just no pretending you are anywhere but in a "concrete jungle" as my grandfather says.

The twenty-yard dash takes all of two minutes 'cause most of the little kids don't know no better than to run off the track or run the wrong way or run smack into the fence and fall down and cry. One little kid, though, has got the good sense to run straight for the white ribbon up ahead so he wins. Then the second-graders line up for the thirty-yard dash and I don't even bother to turn my head to watch 'cause Raphael Perez always wins. He wins before he even begins by psyching the runners, telling them they're going to trip on their shoelaces and fall on their faces or lose their shorts or something, which he doesn't really have to do since he is very fast, almost as fast as I am. After that is the forty-yard dash, which I used to run when I was in first grade. Raymond is hollering from the swings 'cause he knows I'm about to do my thing 'cause the man on the loudspeaker has just announced the fifty-yard dash, although he might just as well be giving a recipe for angel food cake 'cause you can hardly make out what he's saying for the static. I get up and slip off my sweat pants and then I see Gretchen standing at the starting line, kicking her legs out like a pro. Then as I get into place I see that ole Raymond is on line on the other side of the fence, bending down with his fingers on the ground just like he knew what he was doing. I was going to yell at him but then I didn't. It burns up your energy to holler.

Every time, just before I take off in a race, I always feel like I'm in a dream, the kind of dream you have when you're sick with fever and feel all hot and weightless. I dream I'm flying over a sandy beach in the early morning sun, kissing the leaves of the trees as I fly by. And there's always the smell of apples, just like in the country when I was little and used to think I was a choo-choo train, running through the fields of corn and chugging up the hill to the orchard. And all the time I'm dreaming this, I get lighter and lighter until I'm flying over the beach again, getting blown through the sky like a feather that weighs nothing at all. But once I spread my fingers in the dirt and crouch over the Get on Your Mark, the dream goes and I am solid again and am telling myself, Squeaky, you must win, you must win, you are the fastest thing in the world, you can even beat your father up Amsterdam if you really try. And then I feel my weight coming back just behind my knees then down to my feet then into the earth and the pistol shot explodes in my blood and I am off and weightless again, flying past the other runners, my arms pumping up and down and the whole world is quiet except for the crunch as I zoom over the gravel in the track. I glance to my left and there is no one. To the right, a blurred Gretchen, who's got her chin jutting out as if it would win the race all by itself. And on the other side of the fence is Raymond with his arms down to his side and the palms tucked up behind him, running in his very own style, and it's the first time I ever saw that and I almost stop to watch my brother Raymond on his first run. But the white ribbon is bouncing toward me and I tear past it, racing into the distance till my feet with a mind of their own start digging up footfuls of dirt and brake me short. Then all the kids standing on the side pile on me, banging me on the back and slapping my head with their May Day programs, for I have won again and everybody on 151st Street can walk tall for another year.

"In first place . . ." the man on the loudspeaker is clear as a bell now. But then he pauses and the loudspeaker starts to whine. Then static. And I lean down to catch my breath and here comes Gretchen walking back, for she's overshot the finish line, too, huffing and puffing with her hands on her hips taking it slow, breathing in steady time like a real pro, and I sort of like her a little for the first time. "In first place . . ." and then three or four voices get all mixed up on the loudspeaker and I dig my sneaker into the grass and stare at Gretchen, who's staring back, we both wondering just who did win. I can hear old Beanstalk arguing with the man on the loudspeaker and then a few others running their mouths about what the stopwatches say. Then I hear Raymond yanking at the fence to call me and I wave to shush him, but he keeps rattling the fence like a gorilla in a cage like in them gorilla movies, but then like a dancer or something he starts climbing up nice and easy but very fast. And it occurs to me, watching how smoothly he climbs hand over hand and remembering how he looked running with his arms down to his side and with the wind pulling his mouth back and his teeth showing and all, it occurred to me that Raymond would make a very fine runner. Doesn't he always keep up with me on my trots? And he surely knows how to breathe in counts of seven 'cause he's always doing it at the dinner table, which drives my brother George up the wall. And I'm smiling to beat the band 'cause if I've lost this race, or if me and Gretchen tied, or even if I've won, I can always retire as a runner and begin a whole new career as a coach with Raymond as my champion. After all, with a little more study I can beat Cynthia and her phony self at the spelling bee. And if I bugged my mother, I could get piano lessons and become a star. And I have a big rep as the baddest thing around. And I've got a roomful of ribbons and medals and awards. But what has Raymond got to call his own?

So I stand there with my new plans, laughing out loud by this time as Raymond jumps down from the fence and runs over with his teeth showing and his arms down to the side, which no one before him has quite mastered as a running style. And by the time he comes over I'm jumping up and down so glad to see him — my brother Raymond, a great runner in the family tradition. But of course everyone thinks I'm jumping up and down because the men on the loudspeaker have finally gotten themselves together and compared notes and are announcing, "In first place — Miss Hazel Elizabeth Deborah Parker." (Dig that.) "In second place — Miss Gretchen P. Lewis." And I look over at Gretchen, wondering what the *P* stands for. And I smile. 'Cause she's good, no doubt about it. Maybe she'd like to help me coach Raymond; she obviously is serious about running, as any fool can see. And she nods to congratulate me and then she smiles. And I smile. We stand there with this big smile of respect between us. It's about as real a smile as girls can do for each other, considering we don't practice real smiling every day, you know, 'cause maybe we too busy being flowers or fairies or strawberries instead of something honest and worthy of re-spect . . . you know . . . like being people.

A Boy and His Dog

Martha Brooks

My dog is old. And he farts a lot. His eyes are constantly runny on account of he's going blind. Sometimes when we go for his walk he falls down. We'll be moving right along, I'll feel an unexpected tug at his leash and bingo! he's over. The first time it happened he cried, sort of whimpered, and looked at his leg, the back one, the one that had betrayed him. I crouched in the tall grass (we take our walks in a sky-filled prairie field near the townhouses where we live) and felt the leg, which was in a spasm. I told him if it didn't work too well to just give up for a while. He seemed to know what I was telling him because he looked at me, whimpered some more, and finally flopped his head back on my leg. That's what kills me about dogs. They figure you're in charge of everything. Like if you pointed your finger, you could make a house fall down. Or if you told them everything's going to be okay, it would be.

After a couple of minutes he stood up and took off again in that businesslike, let's-get-the-show-on-the-road manner of his, sniffing, squatting to pee (he doesn't lift his leg anymore) near every bush in sight. Later, I found out he fell over because of arthritis. "Nothing you can do, really," said the vet, patting Alphonse's broad flat head. "He's just getting old, Buddy." She gave me some red pellet-shaped arthritis pills and sent us home.

After that, whenever he fell, he'd look quite cheerful. He'd lick the leg a bit, hang out his tongue, pant, and patiently wait. Just before stumbling to his feet, he'd look up like he was saying thank you — when I hadn't done anything!

I couldn't let him see how bad all this made me feel. He's so smart sometimes you have to put your hands over his ears and spell things so he won't know what you're talking about. Things like cheese, cookie, walk. All his favorites.

Mom said, "He can't last forever. Everybody dies sooner or later. It's the natural course of events. And big dogs don't live as long as little dogs."

Around our house, nobody put their hands over my ears.

Alphonse was a present for my first birthday. Dad brought him home, just a scruffy little brown pup someone was giving away. No special breed. I still have a snapshot of him and me at the party. I was this goopy-looking blond kid in blue corduroy overalls and a Donald Duck T-shirt. Alphonse was all over me in the way of puppies. I'd been startled by Dad's flash and also by Alphonse, who'd chosen that exact moment to paw me down and slurp strawberry ice cream off my face and hands. Dad says I didn't cry or anything! Just lay bug-eyed on the shag rug with Alphonse wiggling and slopping all over me. We got on like a house on fire after that.

Which is why it's so unfair that I'm fourteen going on fifteen and he's thirteen going on ninety-four.

I guess I thought we'd just go on forever with Alphonse being my dog. Listening when I tell him stuff. When he goes, who am I going to tell my secrets to? I tell him things I wouldn't even tell Herb Malken, who is my best friend now that we've been in this city a year. My dad's always getting transferred. He's in the army. When I grow up that's one thing I'm not going to be. In the army. I won't make my kids move every three years and leave all their friends behind. Which is one thing I *am* going to do: have more than one kid when I get married.

There's a big myth that only children are selfish and self-centered. I can say from personal experience that only children are more likely to feel guilty and be too eager to please. It's terrible when you are one kid having to be everything to two parents.

Which is why Alphonse is more than just a dog, you see. Mom even sometimes calls him "Baby." Like he's my brother. Which it sometimes feels like.

Last week he had bad gas. I always sleep with the windows open. Even so, it got pretty awful in my bedroom.

Alphonse doesn't make much sound when he farts. Just a little "phhhht" like a balloon with a slow leak and there's no living with him. I swear when he gets like that it would be dangerous to light a match.

I sent him out. He went obligingly. He's always been a polite dog. I listened, first to his toenails clicking over the hardwood floors, then to the scratching of his dry bristly fur as he slumped against the other side of the bedroom door. When you can't be in the same room with someone who's shared your dreams for thirteen years, it's hard to get properly relaxed. It isn't the same when they aren't near you, breathing the same air.

For the next few days he lay around more than usual. I thought perhaps he was just overtired (even though I hadn't been able to stand it and had begun to let him back into my room, farts and all). By Sunday, Mom cocked her head at him and said to Dad and me, "I don't like the way Alphonse looks. Better take him back to the vet, Buddy."

Mom works at the army base too. It's late when she and Dad get home and by that time the vet is closed for the day. So I always take Alphonse right after school. It isn't far — three blocks past the field.

Monday was the kind of fall day that makes you breathe more deeply — the field all burning colors, far-off bushes little flames of magenta and orange, dry wavy grass a pale yellow, and the big sky that kind of deep fire blue you see only once a year, in October. Alphonse didn't fall down once. Eyes half closed, he walked slowly, sniffing the air to take in messages.

A young ginger-colored cat slithered under a wooden fence and into the field. It saw Alphonse and suddenly crouched low, eyes dark, motionless. For a minute there I didn't think he would notice it. Then his ears went up and his head shot forward. Next thing, he was hauling me along at the end of his leash, barking himself into a frenzy. The cat parted the grass like wildfire and, reaching the fence, dug its body grace-lessly under at a spot where there seemed hardly an inch between wood and solid earth.

Alphonse has that effect on cats. They must think he's death on wheels the way they scatter to get out of his way. He stared proudly in the direction of the fence; his nose hadn't failed him. He walked on, a little more vigor in his step, his tongue lolling out, his ears nice and perky.

We reached the edge of the field where we usually turn around on our walks. This time, of course, we didn't. He lost some of his bounce and trailed slightly behind. I looked back. He lowered his head. "She's not going to do anything to you, you crazy dog," I told him. "She's going to shake her head again, and tell us to go home." He kept pace with me after that. Like I said, dogs believe everything you tell them.

The vet is the kind of person whose job runs her life. One minute she's smiling over a recovering patient, or one who's come in just for shots; the next, she's blowing her nose like the place is a funeral parlor. It must be murder to become so involved with your patients. She always looks as if she needs someplace to hole up for a good sleep. And her legs are mag- nets for strays who are forever up for adoption.

At the clinic, I sat down with Alphonse resignedly backed up between my knees. To my astonishment, a resident cat sauntered over and actually rubbed against him. Alphonse sniffed its head and then ignored it (he only likes cats who run). He watched the door to the examining room and trem- bled. I wondered if his eyesight was improving. With one hand I held his leash; the other I bit away at because of hangnails.

When the vet, smiling, summoned us, I got to my feet and Alphonse reluctantly pattered after me. Inside the examining room he pressed against the door, willing it to open. I picked him up and lugged him over to the table.

"He's lost weight," said the vet, stroking, prodding gently.

"He was too fat," I said, patting his stomach.

She laughed, continuing her way down his body. "Has he been on a diet?"

"No. I guess older dogs don't eat as much — like older people."

She looked at his rectum. "How long has this been here?" she said softly, more to herself than to me.

"This what?" I looked.

"It's quite a small lump," she said, pressing it hard.

Alphonse stood politely on the table, shaking and puffing.

"Sometimes," she said, with a reassuring smile, "older dogs

get these lumps and they usually aren't anything to worry about, Buddy."

Usually? What did she mean, *usually*? My heart began to race.

"Older neutered dogs," she continued, in the same even tone, "very often get benign lumps in the anal region. But we'd better check this out, anyway. . . ."

My dog has cancer. What do I tell him now? What am I going to do? Mom and Dad have left it up to me. The vet, with strained sad eyes, said the little lump is just a symptom of what's going on inside. Why didn't I notice that he was so short of breath? That he was peeing more than usual? That he didn't eat much? That his bowels weren't working? She tells me that when dogs are old all of these things become a problem, it's the usual progress of aging. Except not in Alphonse's case. But how would I know that? I shouldn't blame myself. She says there was nothing I could have done to stop it, anyway.

So what do I tell him? Is he in pain? I couldn't stand it if he were in pain. Tonight Mom wanted to give me a sleeping pill. I refused it. Alphonse is here with me on my bed. He's going to sleep with me one last time. I'll hold him and tell him about me and what I plan to do with my life. I'll have to lie a little, fill in a few places, because I'm not *exactly* sure. But he has a right to know what he'll be missing. I'll have a good life, I know it, just like he's had. I'm going to tell him about it now, whisper it in his ear, and I won't leave out a single detail.

The Alligators

John Updike

Joan Edison came to their half of the fifth grade from Maryland in March. She had a thin face with something of a grown-up's tired expression and long black eyelashes like a doll's. Everybody hated her. That month Miss Fritz was reading to them during homeroom about a girl, Emmy, who was badly spoiled and always telling her parents lies about her twin sister, Annie; nobody could believe, it was too amazing, how exactly when they were despising Emmy most, Joan should come into the school with her show-off clothes and her hair left hanging down the back of her fuzzy sweater instead of being cut or braided and her having the crust to actually argue with teachers. "Well I'm sorry," she told Miss Fritz, not even rising from her seat, "but I *don't* see what the point is of homework. In Baltimore we never had any, and the *little* kids there knew what's in these books."

Charlie, who in a way enjoyed homework, was ready to join in the angry moan of the others. Little hurt lines had leapt up between Miss Fritz's eyebrows and he felt sorry for her, remembering how when that September John Eberly had half on-purpose spilled purple Sho-Card paint on the newly sandpapered floor, she had hidden her face in her arms on the desk and cried. She was afraid of the school board. "You're not in Baltimore now, Joan," Miss Fritz said. "You are in Olinger, Pennsylvania."

The children, Charlie among them, laughed, and Joan, blushing a soft brown color and raising her voice excitedly against the current of hatred, got in deeper by trying to explain. "Like there, instead of just *reading* about plants in a book, we'd one day all bring in a flower we'd *picked* and cut it open and look at in a *microscope*." Because of her saying this, shadows, of broad leaves and wild slashed foreign flowers, darkened and complicated the idea they had of her.

Miss Fritz puckered her orange lips into fine wrinkles, then smiled. "In the upper levels you will be allowed to do that in this school. All things come in time, Joan, to patient little girls." When Joan started to argue *this*, Miss Fritz lifted one finger and said with the extra weight adults always have, held back in reserve, "No. No more, young lady, or you'll be in *serious* trouble with me." It gave the class courage to see that Miss Fritz didn't like her either.

After that, Joan couldn't open her mouth in class without there being a great groan. Outdoors on the macadam playground, at recess or fire drill or waiting in the morning for the buzzer, hardly anybody talked to her except to say "Stuck-up" or "Emmy" or "Whore, whore, from Balti-more." Boys were always yanking open the bow at the back of her fancy dresses and flipping little spitballs into the curls of her hanging hair. Once John Eberly even cut a section of her hair off with a yellow plastic scissors stolen from art class. This was the one time Charlie saw Joan cry actual tears. He was as bad as the others: worse, because what the others did because they felt like it, he did out of a plan, to make himself more popular. In the first and second grade he had been liked pretty well, but somewhere since then he had been dropped. There was a gang, boys and girls both, that met Saturdays — you heard them talk about it on Mondays — in Stuart Morrison's garage, and took hikes and played touch football together, and in winter sledded on Hill Street, and in spring bicycled all over Olinger and did together what else, he couldn't imagine. Charlie had known the chief members since before kindergarten. But after school there seemed nothing for him to do but go home promptly and do his homework and fiddle with his Central American stamps and go to horror movies alone, and on weekends nothing but beat monotonously at marbles or Monopoly or chess Darryl Johns or Marvin Auerbach, who he wouldn't have bothered at all with if they hadn't lived right in the neighborhood, they being at least a year younger and not bright for their age, either. Charlie thought the gang might notice him and take him in if he backed up their policies without being asked.

In Science, which 5A had in Miss Brobst's room across the hall, he sat one seat ahead of Joan and annoyed her all he could, in spite of a feeling that, both being disliked, they had something to share. One fact he discovered was she wasn't that bright. Her marks on quizzes were always lower than his. He told her, "Cutting up all those flowers didn't do you much good. Or maybe in Baltimore they taught you everything so long ago you've forgotten it in your old age."

Charlie drew; on his tablet where she could easily see over his shoulder he once in a while drew a picture titled "Joan the Dope": the profile of a girl with a lean nose and sad mince-mouth, the lashes of her lowered eye as black as the pencil could make them and the hair falling, in ridiculous hooks, row after row, down through the sea-blue cross-lines clear off the bottom edge of the tablet.

March turned into spring. One of the signals was, on the high-school grounds, before the cinder track was weeded and when the softball field was still four inches of mud, Happy Lasker came with the elaborate airplane model he had wasted the winter making. It had the American star on the wingtips and a pilot painted inside the cockpit and a miniature motor that burned real gas. The buzzing, off and on all Saturday morning, collected smaller kids from Second Street down to Lynoak. Then it was always the same: Happy shoved the plane into the air, where it climbed and made a razzing noise a minute, then nose-dived and crashed and usually burned in the grass or mud. Happy's father was rich.

In the weeks since she had come, Joan's clothes had slowly grown simpler, to go with the other girls', and one day she came to school with most of her hair cut off, and the rest brushed flat around her head and brought into a little tail behind. The laughter at her was more than she had ever heard. "Ooh. Baldy-paldy!" some idiot girl had exclaimed when Joan came into the cloakroom, and the stupid words went sliding around class all morning. "Baldy-paldy from Baltimore. Why is old Baldy-paldy red in the face?" John Eberly kept making the motion of a scissors with his fingers and its juicy ticking sound with his tongue. Miss Fritz rapped her knuckles on the windowsill until she was rubbing the ache with the other hand, and finally she sent two boys to Mr. Lengel's office, delighting Charlie an enormous secret amount.

His own reaction to the haircut had been quiet, to want to draw her, changed. He had kept the other drawings folded in his desk, and one of his instincts was toward complete sets of things, Batman comics and A's and Costa Rican stamps. Halfway across the room from him, Joan held very still, afraid, it seemed, to move even a hand, her face a shade pink. The haircut had brought out her forehead and exposed her neck and made her chin pointier and her eyes larger. Charlie felt thankful once again for having been born a boy, and having no sharp shocks, like losing your curls or starting to bleed, to make growing painful. How much girls suffer had been one of the first thoughts he had ever had. His caricature of her was wonderful, the work of a genius. He showed it to Stuart Morrison behind him; it was too good for him to appreciate, his dull egg eyes just flickered over it. Charlie traced it onto another piece of tablet paper, making her head completely bald. This drawing Stuart grabbed and it was passed clear around the room.

That night he had the dream. He must have dreamed it while lying there asleep in the morning light, for it was fresh in his head when he woke. They had been in a jungle. Joan, dressed in a torn sarong, was swimming in a clear river among alligators. Somehow, as if from a tree, he was looking down, and there was a calmness in the way the slim girl and the green alligators moved, in and out, perfectly visible under the window-skin of the water. Joan's face sometimes showed the horror she was undergoing and sometimes looked numb. Her hair trailed behind and fanned when her face came toward the surface. He shouted silently with grief. Then he had rescued her; without a sense of having dipped his arms in water, he was carrying her in two arms, himself in a bathing suit, and his feet firmly fixed to the knobby back of an alligator which skimmed upstream, through the shadows of high trees and white flowers and hanging vines, like a surfboard in a movie short. They seemed to be heading toward a wooden bridge arching over the stream. He wondered how he would duck it, and the river and the jungle gave way to his bed and his room, but through the change persisted, like a pedalled note on a piano, the sweetness and pride he had felt in saving and carrying the girl.

He loved Joan Edison. The morning was rainy, and under the umbrella his mother made him take this new knowledge, repeated again and again to himself, gathered like a bell of smoke. Love had no taste, but sharpened his sense of smell so that his oilcloth coat, his rubber boots, the red-tipped bushes hanging over the low walls holding back lawns all along Grand Street, even the dirt and moss in the cracks of the pavement each gave off clear odors. He would have laughed, if a wooden weight had not been placed high in his chest, near where his throat joined. He could not imagine himself laughing soon. It seemed he had reached one of those situations his Sunday-school teacher, poor Miss West with her little moustache, had been trying to prepare him for. He prayed, *Give me Joan*. With the wet weather a solemn flatness had fallen over everything; an orange bus turning at the Bend and four birds on a telephone wire seemed to have the same importance. Yet he felt firmer and lighter and felt things as edges he must whip around and channels he must rush down. If he carried her off, did rescue her from the others' cruelty, he would have defied the gang and made a new one, his own. Just Joan and he at first, then others escaping from meanness and dumbness, until his gang was stronger and Stuart Morrison's garage was empty every Saturday. Charlie would be a king, with his own touch-football game. Everyone would come and plead with him for mercy.

His first step was to tell all those in the cloakroom he loved Joan Edison now. They cared less than he had expected, considering how she was hated. He had more or less expected to have to fight with his fists. Hardly anybody gathered to hear the dream he had pictured himself telling everybody.

Anyway, that morning it would go around the class that he said he loved her, and though this was what he wanted, to in a way open a space between him and Joan, it felt funny nevertheless, and he stuttered when Miss Fritz had him go to the blackboard to explain something.

At lunch, he deliberately hid in the variety store until he saw her walk by. The homely girl with her, he knew, turned off at the next street. He waited a minute and then came out and began running to overtake Joan in the block between the street where the other girl turned down and the street where he turned up. It had stopped raining, and his rolled-up umbrella felt like a commando's bayonet. Coming up behind her, he said, "Bang. Bang."

She turned, and under her gaze, knowing she knew he loved her, his face heated and he stared down. "Why, Charlie," her voice said with her Maryland slowness, "what are you doing on this side of the street?" Carl the town cop stood in front of the elementary school to get them on the side of Grand Street where they belonged. Now Charlie would have to cross the avenue again, by himself, at the dangerous five-spoked intersection.

"Nothing," he said, and used up the one sentence he had prepared ahead: "I like your hair the new way."

"Thank you," she said, and stopped. In Baltimore she must have had manner lessons. Her eyes looked at his, and his vision jumped back from the rims of her lower lids as if from a brink. Yet in the space she occupied there was a great fullness that lent him height, as if he were standing by a window giving on the first morning after a snow.

"But then I didn't mind it the old way either."

"Yes?"

A peculiar reply. Another peculiar thing was the tan beneath her skin; he had noticed before, though not so closely, how when she colored it came up a gentle dull brown more than red. Also she wore something perfumed.

He asked, "How do you like Olinger?"

"Oh, I think it's nice."

"Nice? I guess. I guess maybe. Nice Olinger. I wouldn't know because I've never been anywhere else."

She luckily took this as a joke and laughed. Rather than risk saying something unfunny, he began to balance the umbrella by its point on one finger and, when this went well, walked backwards, shifting the balanced umbrella, its hook black against the patchy blue sky, from one palm to the other, back and forth. At the corner where they parted he got carried away and in imitating a suave gent leaning on a cane bent the handle hopelessly. Her amazement was worth twice the price of his mother's probable crossness.

He planned to walk her again, and farther, after school. All through lunch he kept calculating. His father and he would repaint his bike. At the next haircut he could have his hair parted on the other side to get away from his cowlick. He would change himself totally; everyone would wonder what had happened to him. He would learn to swim, and take her to the dam.

In the afternoon the momentum of the dream wore off somewhat. Now that he kept his eyes always on her, he noticed, with a qualm of his stomach, that in passing in the afternoon from Miss Brobst's to Miss Fritz's room, Joan was not alone, but chattered with others. In class, too, she whispered. So it was with more shame — such shame that he didn't believe he could ever face even his parents again — than surprise that from behind the dark pane of the variety store he saw her walk by in the company of the gang, she and Stuart Morrison throwing back their teeth and screaming and he imitating something and poor moronic John Eberly tagging behind like a thick tail. Charlie watched them walk out of sight behind a tall hedge; relief was as yet a tiny fraction of his reversed world. It came to him that what he had taken for cruelty had been love, that far from hating her everybody had loved her from the beginning, and that even the stupidest knew it weeks before he did. That she was the queen of the class and might as well not exist, for all the good he would get out of it.

Celia Behind Me

Isabel Huggan

There was a little girl with large smooth cheeks and very thick glasses who lived up the street when I was in public school. Her name was Celia. It was far too rare and grown-up a name, so we always laughed at it. And we laughed at her because she was a chubby, diabetic child, made peevish by our teasing.

My mother always said, "You must be nice to Celia — she won't live forever," and even as early as seven I could see the unfairness of that position. Everybody died sooner or later, I'd die too, but that didn't mean everybody was nice to me or to each other. I already knew about mortality and was prepared to go to heaven with my two aunts who had died together in a car crash with their heads smashed like overripe melons. I overheard the bit about the melons when my mother was on the telephone, repeating that phrase and sobbing. I used to think about it often, repeating the words to myself as I did other things so that I got a nice rhythm: "Their heads smashed like melons, like melons, like melons." I imagined the pulpy insides of muskmelons and watermelons all over the road.

I often thought about the melons when I saw Celia because

her head was so round and she seemed so bland and stupid
and fruitlike. All rosy and vulnerable at the same time as
being the most *awful* pain. She'd follow us home from school,
whining if we walked faster than she did. Everybody always
walked faster than Celia because her short little legs wouldn't
keep up. And she was bundled in long stockings and heavy
underwear, summer and winter, so that even her clothes held
her back from our sturdy, leaping pace over and under hedges
and across backyards and, when it was dry, or when it was
frozen, down the stream bed and through the drainage pipe
beneath the bridge on Church Street.

Celia, by the year I turned nine in December, had failed
once and was behind us in school, which was a relief because
at least in class there wasn't someone telling you to be nice
to Celia. But she'd always be in the playground at recess, her
pleading eyes magnified behind those ugly lenses so that you
couldn't look at her when you told her she couldn't play
skipping unless she was an ender. "Because you can't skip
worth a fart," we'd whisper in her ear. "Fart, fart, fart," and
watch her round pink face crumple as she stood there, turning, turning, turning the rope over and over.

As the fall turned to winter, the five of us who lived on
Brubacher Street and went back and forth to school together
got meaner and meaner to Celia. And, after the brief diver-
sions of Christmas, we returned with a vengeance to our running and hiding and scaring games that kept Celia in a state
of terror all the way home.

My mother said, one day when I'd come into the kitchen
and she'd just turned away from the window so I could see
she'd been watching us coming down the street, "You'll be
sorry, Elizabeth. I see how you're treating that poor child,
and it makes me sick. You wait, young lady. Some day you'll
see how it feels yourself. Now you be nice to her, d'you hear?"

"But it's not just me," I protested. "I'm nicer to her than anybody else, and I don't see why I have to be. She's nobody special, she's just a pain. She's really dumb and she can't do anything. Why can't I just play with the other kids like everybody else?"

"You just remember I'm watching," she said, ignoring every word I'd said. "And if I see one more snowball thrown in her direction, by you or by anybody else, I'm coming right out there and spanking you in front of them all. Now you remember that!"

I knew my mother, and knew this was no idle threat. The awesome responsibility of now making sure the other kids stopped snowballing Celia made me weep with rage and despair, and I was locked in my room after supper to "think things over."

I thought things over. I hated Celia with a dreadful and absolute passion. Her round guileless face floated in the air above me as I finally fell asleep, taunting me: "You have to be nice to me because I'm going to die."

I did as my mother bid me, out of fear and the thought of the shame that a public spanking would bring. I imagined my mother could see much farther up the street than she really could, and it prevented me from throwing snowballs or teasing Celia for the last four blocks of our homeward journey. And then came the stomach-wrenching task of making the others quit.

"You'd better stop," I'd say. "If my mother sees you she's going to thrash us all."

Terror of terrors that they wouldn't be sufficiently scared of her strap-wielding hand; gut-knotting fear that they'd find out or guess what she'd really said and throw millions of snowballs just for the joy of seeing me whipped, pants down in the snowbank, screaming. I visualized that scene all winter, and felt a shock of relief when March brought such a cold spell that the snow was too crisp for packing. It meant a temporary safety for Celia, and respite for me. For I knew, deep in my wretched heart, that were it not for Celia I was next in line for humiliation. I was kind of chunky and wore glasses too, and had sucked my thumb so openly in kindergarten that "Sucky" had stuck with me all the way to Grade 3, where I now balanced at a hazardous point, nearly accepted by the amorphous Other Kids and always at the brink of being laughed at, ignored, or teased. I cried very easily, and prayed during those years — not to become pretty or smart or popular, all aims too far out of my or God's reach, but simply to be strong enough not to cry when I got called Sucky.

During that cold snap, we were all bundled up by our mothers as much as poor Celia ever was. Our comings and goings were hampered by layers of flannel bloomers and undershirts and ribbed stockings and itchy wool against us no matter which way we turned; mitts, sweaters, scarves and hats, heavy and wet-smelling when the snot from our dripping noses mixed with the melting snow on our collars, and we wiped, in frigid resignation, our sore red faces with rough sleeves knobbed over with icy pellets.

Trudging, turgid little beasts we were, making our way along slippery streets, breaking the crusts on those few front yards we'd not yet stepped all over in glee to hear the glorious snapping sound of boot through hard snow. Celia, her glasses steamed up even worse than mine, would scuffle and trip a few yards behind us, and I walked along wishing that sometime I'd look back and she wouldn't be there. But she always was, and I was always conscious of the abiding hatred that had built up during the winter, in conflict with other emotions that gave me no peace at all. I felt pity, and a rising urge within me to cry as hard as I could so that Celia would cry too, and somehow realize how bad she made me feel, and ask my forgiveness.

It was the last day before the thaw when the tension broke, like northern lights exploding in the frozen air. We were all a little wingy after days of switching between the extremes of bitter cold outdoors and the heat of our homes and school. Thermostats had been turned up in a desperate attempt to combat the arctic air, so that we children suffered scratchy, tingly torment in our faces, hands, and feet as the blood in our bodies roared in confusion, first freezing, then boiling. At school we had to go outside at recess — only an act of God would have ever prevented recess; the teachers had to have their cigarettes and tea — and in bad weather we huddled in a shed where the bicycles and the janitor's outdoor equipment were stored.

During the afternoon recess of the day I'm remembering, at the end of the shed where the girls stood, a sudden commotion broke out when Sandra, a rich big girl from Grade 4, brought forth a huge milk-chocolate bar from her pocket. It was brittle in the icy air, and snapped into little bits in its foil wrapper, to be divided among the chosen. I made my way cautiously to the fringe of her group, where many of my classmates were receiving their smidgens of sweet chocolate, letting it melt on their tongues like dark communion wafers. Behind me hung Celia, who had mistaken my earlier cries of "Stop throwing snowballs at Celia!" for kindness. She'd been mooning behind me for days, it seemed to me, as I stepped a little farther forward to see that there were only a few pieces left. Happily, though, most mouths were full and the air hummed with the murmuring sound of chocolate being pressed between tongue and palate.

Made bold by cold and desire, I spoke up. "Could I have a bit, Sandra?" She turned to where Celia and I stood, holding the precious foil in her mittened hand. Wrapping it in a ball, she pushed it over at Celia. Act of kindness, act of spite, vicious bitch, or richness seeking expiation? She gave the chocolate to Celia and smiled at her. "This last bit is for Celia," she said to me.

"But I can't eat it," whispered Celia, her round red face aflame with the sensation of being singled out for a gift. "I've got di-a-beet-is." The word. Said so carefully. As if it were a talisman, a charm to protect her against our rough health-iness.

I knew it was a trick. I knew she was watching me out of the corner of her eye, that Sandra, but I was driven. "Then could I have it, eh?" The duress under which I acted prompted my chin to quiver and a tear to start down my cheek before I could wipe it away.

"No, no, no!" jeered Sandra then. "Suckybabies can't have sweets either. Di-a-beet-ics and Suck-y-ba-bies can't eat choc-olate. Give it back, you little fart, Celia! That's the last time I ever give you anything!"

Wild, appreciative laughter from the chocolate-tongued mob, and they turned their backs on us, Celia and me, and waited while Sandra crushed the remaining bits into minus-cule slivers. They had to take off their mitts and lick their fingers to pick up the last fragments from the foil. I stood there and prayed: "Dear God and Jesus, I would please like very much not to cry. Please help me. Amen." And with that the clanging recess bell clanked through the playground noise, and we all lined up, girls and boys in straight, straight rows, to go inside.

After school there was the usual bunch of us walking home and, of course, Celia trailing behind us. The cold of the past few days had been making us hurry, taking the shortest routes on our way to steaming cups of Ovaltine and cocoa. But this day we were all full of that peculiar energy that swells up before a turn in the weather and, as one body, we turned down the street that meant the long way home. Past the feed store where the Mennonites tied their horses, out the back of the town hall parking lot and then down a ridge to the ice-covered stream and through the Church Street culvert to come out in the unused field behind the Front Street stores; the forbidden adventure we indulged in as a gesture of defiance against the parental "come right home."

We slid down the snowy slope at the mouth of the pipe that seemed immense then but was really only five feet in diameter. Part of its attraction was the tremendous racket you could make by scraping a stick along the corrugated sides as you went through. It was also long enough to echo very nicely if you made good booming noises, and we occasionally titillated each other by saying bad words at one end that grew as they bounced along the pipe and became wonderfully shocking in their magnitude . . . poopy, Poopy, POOpy, POOOOPy, POOOOPPYYY!

I was last because I had dropped my schoolbag in the snow and stopped to brush it off. And when I looked up, down at the far end, where the white plate of daylight lay stark in the darkness, the figures of my four friends were silhouetted as they emerged into the brightness. As I started making great sliding steps to catch up, I heard Celia behind me, and her plaintive, high voice: "Elizabeth! Wait for me, okay? I'm scared to go through alone. Elizabeth?"

And of course I slid faster and faster, unable to stand the thought of being the only one in the culvert with Celia. Then we would come out together and we'd really be paired up. What if they always ran on ahead and left us to walk together? What would I ever do? And behind me I heard the rising call of Celia, who had ventured as far as a few yards into the pipe, calling my name to come back and walk with her. I got right to the end, when I heard another noise and looked up. There they all were, on the bridge looking down, and as soon as they saw my face began to chant, "Better wait for Celia, Sucky. Better get Celia, Sucky."

The sky was very pale and lifeless, and I looked up in the air at my breath curling in spirals and felt, I remember this very well, an exhilarating, clear-headed instant of understanding. And with that, raced back into the tunnel, where Celia stood whimpering halfway along.

"You little fart!" I screamed at her, my voice breaking and tearing at the words. "You little diabetic fart! I hate you! I hate you! Stop it, stop crying, I hate you! I could bash your head in I hate you so much, you fart, you fart! I'll smash your head like a melon! And it'll go in pieces all over and you'll die. You'll die, you diabetic. You're going to die!" Shaking her, shaking her and banging her against the cold, ribbed metal, crying and sobbing for grief and gasping with the exertion of pure hatred. And then there were the others, pulling at me, yanking me away, and in the moral tones of those who don't actually take part, warning me that they were going to tell, that Celia probably was going to die now, that I was really evil, they would tell what I said.

And there, slumped in a little heap was Celia, her round head in its furry bonnet all dirty at the back where it had hit against the pipe, and she was hiccupping with fear. And for a wild, terrible moment I thought I had killed her, that the movements and noises her body made were part of dying.

I ran.

I ran as fast as I could back out the way we had come, and all the way back to the schoolyard. I didn't think about where I was going, it simply seemed the only bulwark to turn to when I knew I couldn't go home. There were a few kids still in the yard but they were older and ignored me as I tried the handle of the side door and found it open. I'd never been in the school after hours, and was stricken with another kind of terror that it might be a strappable offense. But no one saw me, even the janitor was blessedly in another part of the building, so I was able to creep down to the girls' washroom and quickly hide in one of the cubicles. Furtive, criminal, condemned.

I was so filled with horror I couldn't even cry. I just sat on the toilet seat, reading all the things that were written in pencil on the green, wooden walls. *G. R. loves M. H. and Y. F. hates W. S. for double double sure. Mr. Becker wears ladies' pants.* Thinking that I might die myself, die right here, and then it wouldn't matter if they told on me that I had killed Celia.

But the inevitable footsteps of retribution came down the stone steps before I had been there very long. I heard the janitor's voice explaining he hadn't seen any children come in and then my father's voice saying that the others were sure this is where Elizabeth would be. And they called my name, and then came in, and I guess saw my boots beneath the door because I suddenly thought it was too late to scrunch them up on the seat and my father was looking down at me and grabbed my arm, hurting it, pulling me, saying "Get in the car, Elizabeth."

Both my mother and my father spanked me that night. At first I tried not to cry, and tried to defend myself against their diatribe, tried to tell them when they asked, "But whatever possessed you to do such a terrible thing?" But whatever I said seemed to make them more angry and they became so soured by their own shame that they slapped my stinging buttocks for personal revenge as much as for any rehabilitative purposes.

"I'll never be able to lift my head on this street again!" my mother cried, and it struck me then, as it still does now, as a marvelous turn of phrase. I thought about her head on the street as she hit me, and wondered what Celia's head looked like, and if I had dented it at all.

Celia hadn't died, of course. She'd been half-carried, half-dragged home by the heroic others, and given pills and attention and love, and the doctor had come to look at her head but she didn't have so much as a bruise. She had a dirty hat, and a bad case of hiccups all night, but she survived.

Celia forgave me, all too soon. Within weeks her mother allowed her to walk back and forth to school with me again. But, in all the years before she finally died at seventeen, I was never able to forgive her. She made me discover a darkness far more frightening than the echoing culvert, far more enduring than her smooth, pink face.

from

This Boy's Life

Tobias Wolff

My friends were Terry Taylor and Terry Silver. All three of us lived with our mothers. Terry Taylor's father was stationed in Korea. The war had been over for two years but he still hadn't come home. Mrs. Taylor had filled the house with pictures of him, graduation portraits, snapshots in and out of uniform — always alone, leaning against trees, standing in front of houses. The living room was like a shrine; if you didn't know better you would have thought that he had not survived Korea but had died some kind of hero's death there, as Mrs. Taylor had perhaps anticipated.

This sepulchral atmosphere owed a lot to the presence of Mrs. Taylor herself. She was a tall, stooped woman with deep-set eyes. She sat in her living room all day long and chain-smoked cigarettes and stared out the picture window with an air of unutterable sadness, as if she knew things beyond mortal bearing. Sometimes she would call Taylor over and wrap her long arms around him, then close her eyes and hoarsely whisper, "Terence! Terence!" Eyes still closed, she would turn her head and resolutely push him away.

Silver and I immediately saw the potential of this scene

and we replayed it often, so often that we could bring tears to Taylor's eyes just by saying "Terence! Terence!" Taylor was a dreamy, thin-skinned boy who cried easily, a weakness from which he tried to distract us by committing acts of ferocious vandalism. He'd once been to juvenile court for breaking windows.

Mrs. Taylor also had two daughters, both older than Terry and full of scorn for us and all our works. "Oh, *God*," they'd say when they saw us. "Look what the cat dragged in." Silver and I suffered their insults meekly, but Taylor always had an answer. "Does your face hurt?" he would say. "I just wondered — it's killing me." "Is that sweater made of camel's hair? I just wondered — I thought I saw two humps."

But they always had the last word. As girls went they were nothing special, but they were girls, and empowered by that fact to render judgment on us. They could make us cringe just by rolling their eyes. Silver and I were afraid of them, and confused by Mrs. Taylor and the funereal atmosphere of the house. The only reason we went there was to steal Mrs. Taylor's cigarettes.

We couldn't go to my place. Phil, the man who owned the boardinghouse, had no use for kids. He rented the room to my mother only after she promised that I would be quiet and never bring other kids home with me. Phil was always there, reeking of chewing tobacco, drooling strings of it into the chipped enamel mug he carried with him everywhere. Phil had been badly burned in a warehouse fire that left his skin blister-smooth and invested with an angry glow, as if the fire still burned somewhere inside him. The fingers of one hand were welded together.

He was right not to want me around. When we passed one another in the hallway or on the stairs, I couldn't keep my eyes from him and he saw in them no sympathy or friendliness, only disgust. He responded by touching me constantly. He knew better but could not help himself. He touched me on the shoulders, on the head, on the neck, using all the gestures of fatherly affection while measuring my horror with a cold bitter gaze, giving new pain to himself as if he had no choice.

My place was off-limits and Terry Taylor's was full of trolls, so we usually ended up at Silver's apartment. Silver was an only child, clever, skinny, malicious, a shameless coward when his big mouth brought trouble down on us. His father was a cantor* who lived in Tacoma with his new wife. Silver's mother worked all day at Boeing. That meant we had the apartment to ourselves for hours at a stretch.

But first we made our rounds. As we left school we followed girls at a safe distance and offered up smart remarks. We drifted in and out of stores, palming anything that wasn't under glass. We coasted stolen tricycles down the hills around Alkai Point, standing on the seats and jumping off at the last moment to send them crashing into parked cars. Sometimes, if we had the money, we took a bus downtown and weaved through the winos around Pioneer Square to stare at guns in the windows of pawnshops. For all three of us the Luger was the weapon of choice; our passion for this pistol was profound and about the only passion we admitted to. In the presence of a Luger we stopped our continual jostling of each other and stood wide-eyed.

Television was very big on the Nazis then. Every week they screened new horrors, always with a somber narrator to remind us that this wasn't make-believe but actual history, that what we were seeing had really happened and could happen again if we did not maintain ourselves in a state of vigilance.

*Chief singer in a synagogue

These shows always ended the same way. Overviews of ruined Berlin. Grinning GIs rousting the defeated Aryan soldiery from their hiding places in barn and cave and sewer. Himmler dead in his cell, hollow-eyed Hess in Spandau. The now lathered-up narrator crowing, "Thus was the high-flying Prussian eagle brought to ground!" and "Thus did the little Führer and his bullyboys turn tail and run, giving up forever their dream of *The Thousand-Year Reich!*"

But these glimpses of humiliation and loss lasted only a few minutes. They were tacked on as a pretense that the point of the show was to celebrate the victory of goodness over evil. We saw through this fraud, of course. We saw that the real point was to celebrate snappy uniforms and racy Mercedes staff cars and great marching, thousands of boots slamming down together on cobbled streets while banners streamed overhead and strong voices sang songs that stirred our blood though we couldn't understand a word. The point was to watch Stukas peel off and dive toward burning cities, tanks blowing holes in buildings, men with Lugers and dogs ordering people around. These shows instructed us further in the faith we were already beginning to hold: that victims are contemptible, no matter how much people pretend otherwise; that it is more fun to be inside than outside, to be arrogant than to be kind, to be with a crowd than to be alone.

Terry Silver had a Nazi armband that he swore was genuine, though anyone could see he'd made it himself. As soon as we reached his apartment Silver would get this armband from its hiding place and slip it on. Then he would strut around and treat Taylor and me like lackeys. We let him do it because of the candy Mrs. Silver left out in crystal bowls, because of the television set, and because without Silver to tell us what to do we were reduced to wandering the sidewalks, listlessly throwing rocks at signs.

First we made a few calls. Taylor and I listened in on the extension in Mrs. Silver's bedroom while Silver did the talking. He looked up people with Jewish-sounding names and screamed at them in pig German. He ordered entire banquets of Chinese food for his father and stepmother. Sometimes he called the parents of kids we didn't like and assumed the voice and manner of a Concerned Adult — teacher, coach, counselor — just touching base to ask whether there was some problem at home that might account for Paul's unusual behavior at school the other day. Silver never laughed, never gave himself away. When he was being particularly plausible and suave, Taylor and I had to stuff Mrs. Silver's coverlet in our mouths and flail the mattress with our fists.

Then, bumping each other with our hips to make room, the three of us would press together in front of Mrs. Silver's full-length mirror to comb our hair and practice looking cool. We wore our hair long at the sides, swept back into a ducktail. The hair on top we combed toward the center and then forward, with spit curls breaking over our foreheads. My mother detested this hairdo and forbade me to wear it, which meant that I wore it everywhere but at home, sustaining the distinctness of two different styles with gobs of Butch Wax that left my hair glossy and hard and my forehead ringed with little pimples.

Unlit cigarettes dangling from the corners of our mouths, eyelids at half mast, we studied ourselves in the mirror. Spit curls. Pants pulled down low on our hips, thin white belts buckled on the side. Shirts with three-quarter-length sleeves. Collars raised behind our necks. We should have looked cool, but we didn't. Silver was emaciated. His eyes bulged, his Adam's apple protruded, his arms poked out of his sleeves like pencils with gloves stuck on the ends. Taylor had the liquid eyes and long lashes and broad blank face of a cow. I didn't look that great myself. But it wasn't really our looks that made us uncool. Coolness did not demand anything as obvious as that. Like chess or music, coolness claimed its own out of some mysterious impulse of recognition. Uncoolness did likewise. We had been claimed by uncoolness.

At five o'clock we turned on the television and watched *The Mickey Mouse Club.* It was understood that we were all holding a giant bone for Annette. This was our excuse for watching the show, and for me it was partly true. I had certain ideas of the greater world that Annette belonged to, and I wanted a place in this world. I wanted it with all the feverish, disabling hunger of first love.

At the end of every show the local station gave an address for Mouseketeer Mail. I had begun writing Annette. At first I described myself in pretty much the same terms as I had in my letters to Alice, who was now very much past tense, with the difference that instead of owning a ranch, my father, Cap'n Wolff, now owned a fleet of fishing boats. I was first mate, myself, and a pretty fair hand at reeling in the big ones. I gave Annette some very detailed descriptions of my contests with the friskier fellows I ran up against. I also invited her to consider the fun to be had in visiting Seattle. I told her we had lots of room. I did not tell her that I was eleven years old.

I got back some chipper official responses encouraging me to start an Annette fan club. In other words, to organize my competition. Fat chance. But when I upped the ante in my letters to her, they stopped sending me anything at all. The Disney Studio must have had a kind of secret service that monitored Mouseketeer Mail for inappropriate sentiments and declarations. When my name went off the mailing list, it probably went onto some other list. But Alice had taught me about coyness. I kept writing Annette and began to imag-

ine a terrible accident in front of her house that would almost
but not quite kill me, leaving me dependent on her care and
sympathy, which in time would turn to admiration, love . . .

As soon as she appeared on the show — "Hi, I'm Annette!"
— Taylor would start moaning and Silver would lick the
screen with his tongue. "Come here, baby," he'd say, "I've
got six inches of piping hot flesh just for you."

We all said things like that — it was a formality — then
we shut up and watched the show. Our absorption was complete. We softened. We surrendered. We joined the club.
Taylor forgot himself and sucked his thumb, and Silver and
I let him get away with it. We watched the Mouseketeers
get all excited about wholesome projects and have wimpy
adventures and talk about their feelings, and we didn't laugh
at them. We didn't laugh at them when they said nice things
about their parents, or when they were polite to each other,
or when they said, "Hey, gang . . ." We watched every minute of it, our eyes glistening in the blue light, and we went
on staring at the television after they had sung the anthem
and faded away into commercials for toothpaste and candy.
Then, blinking and awkward, we would rouse ourselves and
talk dirty about Annette.

Sometimes, when *The Mickey Mouse Club* was over, we
went up to the roof. Silver's apartment building overlooked
California Avenue. Though the street was busy we chose our
targets carefully. Most days we didn't throw anything at all.
But now and then someone would appear who had no chance
of getting past us, like the man in the Thunderbird.

Thunderbirds had been out for only a year now, since '55,
and because they were new and there weren't that many of
them, they were considered somewhat cooler than Corvettes.
It was early evening. The Thunderbird was idling before a red
light at the intersection, and from our perch behind the para-

pet we could hear the song on the radio — "Over the Mountains and across the Seas" — and hear too, just below the music, the full-throated purr of the engine. The black body glistened like obsidian. Blue smoke chugged from the twin exhausts. The top was rolled back. We could see the red leather upholstery and the blond man in the dinner jacket sitting in the driver's seat. He was young and handsome and fresh. You could almost smell the Listerine on his breath, the Mennen on his cheeks. We were looking right down at him. With the palm of his left hand he kept the beat of the song against the steering wheel. His right arm rested on the back of the empty seat beside him, which would not remain empty for long. He was on his way to pick someone up.

We held no conference. One look was enough to see that he was everything we were not, his life a progress of satisfactions we had no hope of attaining in any future we could seriously propose for ourselves.

The first egg hit the street beside him. The second egg hit the front fender. The third egg hit the trunk and splattered his shoulders and neck and hair. We looked down just long enough to tally the damage before pulling our heads back. A moment passed. Then a howl rose skyward. No words — just one solitary soul cry of disbelief. We could still hear the music coming from his radio. The light must have changed, because a horn honked, and honked again, and someone yelled something, and another voice answered harshly, and the song was suddenly lost in the noise of engines.

We rolled back and forth on the roof for a while. Just as we were getting ready to go back down to Silver's apartment, the Thunderbird screeched around the corner up the block. We could hear the driver cursing. The car moved slowly toward the light, combusting loudly. As it passed below we peered over the parapet again. The driver was scanning the sidewalks with stiff angry jerks of his head. He seemed to have no idea where the eggs had come from. We let fly again. One hit the hood with a loud boom, another landed in the seat beside him, the last exploded on the dashboard. Covered with egg and eggshell, he rose in his seat and bellowed.

There was more honking at the light. Again he tore away and again he came back, still bellowing. Six eggs were left in the carton. Each of us took two. Silver knelt by the edge, risking a few hurried glances into the street while holding his arm out behind him to keep us in check until the moment was right. Then he beckoned furiously and we reared up beside him and got rid of our eggs and dropped back out of sight before they hit. The driver was looking up at the building across the street; he never laid eyes on us. We heard the eggs smack the pavement, boom against the car. This time there was no cry of protest. The silence made me uncomfortable and in my discomfort I grinned at Silver, but Silver did not grin back. His face was purple and twitching with anger as if he had been the one set upon and outraged. He was beside himself. Breathing loudly, clenching and unclenching his jaw, he leaned over the edge and cupped his hands in front of his mouth and screamed a word I had heard only once, years before, when my father shouted it at a man who had cut him off in traffic.

"Yid!" Silver screamed, and again, "Yid!"

Priscilla and the Wimps

Richard Peck

Listen, there was a time when you couldn't even go to the *rest room* around this school without a pass. And I'm not talking about those little pink tickets made out by some teacher. I'm talking about a pass that could cost anywhere up to a buck, sold by Monk Klutter.

Not that Mighty Monk ever touched money, not in public. The gang he ran, which ran the school for him, was his collection agency. They were Klutter's Kobras, a name spelled out in nail heads on six well-known black plastic windbreakers.

Monk's threads were more . . . subtle. A pile-lined suede battle jacket with lizard-skin flaps over tailored Levis and a pair of ostrich-skin boots, brassed-toed and suitable for kicking people around. One of his Kobras did nothing all day but walk a half step behind Monk, carrying a fitted bag with Monk's gym shoes, a roll of rest-room passes, a cash box, and a switchblade that Monk gave himself manicures with at lunch over at the Kobras' table.

Speaking of lunch, there were a few cases of advanced malnutrition among the newer kids. The ones who were a little slow in handing over a cut of their lunch money and were therefore barred from the cafeteria. Monk ran a tight ship.

I admit it. I'm five foot five, and when the Kobras slithered by, with or without Monk, I shrank. And I admit this, too: I paid up on a regular basis. And I might add: so would you.

This school was old Monk's Garden of Eden. Unfortunately for him, there was a serpent in it. The reason Monk didn't recognize trouble when it was staring him in the face is that the serpent in the Kobras' Eden was a girl.

Practically every guy in school could show you his scars. Fang marks from Kobras, you might say. And they were all highly visible in the shower room: lumps, lacerations, blue bruises, you name it. But girls usually got off with a warning.

Except there was this one girl named Priscilla Roseberry. Picture a girl named Priscilla Roseberry, and you'll be light years off. Priscilla was, hands down, the largest student in our particular institution of learning. I'm not talking fat. I'm talking big. Even beautiful, in a bionic way. Priscilla wasn't inclined toward organized crime. Otherwise, she could have put together a gang that would turn Klutter's Kobras into garter snakes.

Priscilla was basically a loner except she had one friend. A little guy named Melvin Detweiler. You talk about The Odd Couple. Melvin's one of the smallest guys above midget status ever seen. A really nice guy, but, you know — little. They even had lockers next to each other, in the same bank as mine. I don't know what they had going. I'm not saying this was a romance. After all, people deserve their privacy.

Priscilla was sort of above everything, if you'll pardon a pun. And very calm, as only the very big can be. If there was anybody who didn't notice Klutter's Kobras, it was Priscilla.

Until one winter day after school when we were all grab-

bing our coats out of our lockers. And hurrying, since Klutter's Kobras made sweeps of the halls for after-school shake-
downs.

Anyway, up to Melvin's locker swaggers one of the Kobras.
Never mind his name. Gang members don't need names.
They've got group identity. He reaches down and grabs little
Melvin by the neck and slams his head against his locker
door. The sound of skull against steel rippled all the way
down the locker row, speeding the crowds on their way.

"Okay, let's see your pass," snarls the Kobra.

"A pass for what this time?" Melvin asks, probably still
dazed.

"Let's call it a pass for very short people," says the Kobra,
"a dwarf tax." He wheezes a little Kobra chuckle at his own
wittiness. And already he's reaching for Melvin's wallet with
the hand that isn't circling Melvin's windpipe. All this time,
of course, Melvin and the Kobra are standing in Priscilla's big
shadow.

She's taking her time shoving her books into her locker
and pulling on a very large-size coat. Then, quicker than the
eye, she brings the side of her enormous hand down in a chop
that breaks the Kobra's hold on Melvin's throat. You could
hear a pin drop in that hallway. Nobody'd ever laid a finger
on a Kobra, let alone a hand the size of Priscilla's.

Then Priscilla, who hardly ever says anything to anybody
except to Melvin, says to the Kobra, "Who's your leader,
wimp?"

This practically blows the Kobra away. First he's chopped
by a girl, and now she's acting like she doesn't know Monk
Klutter, the Head Honcho of the World. He's so amazed, he
tells her. "Monk Klutter."

"Never heard of him," Priscilla mentions. "Send him to

see me." The Kobra just backs away from her like the whole situation is too big for him, which it is.

Pretty soon Monk himself slides up. He jerks his head once, and his Kobras slither off down the hall. He's going to handle this interesting case personally. "Who is it around here doesn't know Monk Klutter?"

He's standing inches from Priscilla, but since he'd have to look up at her, he doesn't. "Never heard of him," says Priscilla.

Monk's not happy with this answer, but by now he's spotted Melvin, who's grown smaller in spite of himself. Monk breaks his own rule by reaching for Melvin with his own hands. "Kid," he says, "you're going to have to educate your girl-friend."

His hands never quite make it to Melvin. In a move of pure poetry Priscilla has Monk in a hammerlock. His neck's popping like gunfire, and his head's bowed under the immense weight of her forearm. His suede jacket's peeling back, show-ing pile.

Priscilla's behind him in another easy motion. And with a single mighty thrust forward, frog-marches Monk into her own locker. It's incredible. His ostrich-skin boots click once in the air. And suddenly he's gone, neatly wedged into the locker, a perfect fit. Priscilla bangs the door shut, twirls the lock, and strolls out of school. Melvin goes with her, of course, trotting along below her shoulder. The last stragglers leave quietly.

Well, this is where fate, an even bigger force than Priscilla, steps in. It snows all that night, a blizzard. The whole town ices up. And school closes for a week.

What Means Switch

Gish Jen

There we are, nice Chinese family — father, mother, two born-here girls. Where should we live next? My parents slide the question back and forth like a cup of ginseng neither one wants to drink. Until finally it comes to them. What they really want is a milkshake (chocolate) and to go with it, a house in Scarsdale. What else? The broker tries to hint: the neighborhood, she says. Moneyed. Many delis. Meaning rich and Jewish. But someone has sent my parents a list of the top ten schools nationwide (based on the opinion of selected educators and others) and so, *many-deli* or not, we nestle into a Dutch colonial on the Bronx River Parkway. The road's windy where we are, very charming; drivers miss their turns, plow up our flowerbeds, then want to use our telephone. "Of course," my mom tells them, like it's no big deal, we can replant. We're the type to adjust. You know — the lady drivers weep, my mom gets out the Kleenex for them. We're a bit down the hill from the private plane set, in other words. Only in our dreams do our jacket zippers jam, what with all the lift tickets we have stapled to them, Killington on top of Sugarbush on top of Stowe, and we don't even know where the Virgin Islands are — although certain of us do know that virgins are like priests and nuns, which there were a lot more of in Yonkers, where we just moved from, than there are here.

This is my first understanding of class. In our old neighborhood everybody knew everything about virgins and nonvirgins, not to say the technicalities of staying in-between. Or almost everybody, I should say; in Yonkers I was the laugh-along type. Here I'm an expert.

"You mean the man . . .?" Pigtailed Barbara Gugelstein spits a mouthful of Coke back into her can. "That is *so* gross!"

Pretty soon I'm getting popular for a new girl; the only problem is Danielle Meyers, who wears blue mascara and has gone steady with two boys. "How do *you* know?" she starts to ask, proceeding to edify us all with how she French-kissed one boyfriend and just regular kissed another. ("Because, you know, he had braces.") We hear about his rubber bands, how once one popped right into her mouth. I begin to realize I need to find somebody to kiss too. But how?

Luckily, I just about then happen to tell Barbara Gugelstein I know karate. I don't know why I tell her this. My sister Callie's the liar in the family; ask anybody. I'm the one who doesn't see why we should have to hold our heads up. But for some reason I tell Barbara Gugelstein I can make my hands like steel by thinking hard. "I'm not supposed to tell anyone," I say.

The way she backs away, blinking, I could be the burning bush.

"I can't do bricks," I say — a bit of expectation management. "But I can do your arm if you want." I set my hand in chop position.

"Uhh, it's okay," she says. "I know you can, I saw it on TV last night."

That's when I recall that I too saw it on TV last night — in fact, at her house. I rush on to tell her I know how to get pregnant with tea.

"That's how they do it in China."

She agrees that China is an ancient and great civilization that ought to be known for more than spaghetti and gunpowder. I tell her I know Chinese. *"Be-yeh fa-foon,"* I say. *"Shee-veh. Ji nu."* Meaning, "Stop acting crazy. Rice gruel. Soy sauce." She's impressed. At lunch the next day, Danielle Meyers and Amy Weinstein and Barbara's crush, Andy Kaplan, are all impressed too. Scarsdale is a liberal town, not like Yonkers, where the Whitman Road Gang used to throw crab-apple mash at my sister Callie and me and tell us it would make our eyes stick shut. Here we're like permanent exchange students. In another ten years, there'll be so many Orientals we'll turn into Asians; a Japanese grocery will buy out that one deli too many. But for now, the mid-sixties, what with civil rights on TV, we're not so much accepted as embraced. Especially by the Jewish part of town — which, it turns out, is not all of town at all. That's just an idea people have, Callie says, and lots of them could take us or leave us same as the Christians, who are nice too; I shouldn't generalize. So let me not generalize except to say that pretty soon I've been to so many bar and bas mitzvahs, I can almost say myself whether the kid chants like an angel or like a train conductor, maybe they could use him on the commuter line. At seder I know to forget the bricks, get a good pile of that mortar. Also I know what is schmaltz. I know that I am a goy. This is not why people like me, though. People like me because I do not need to use deodorant, as I demonstrate in the locker room before and after gym. Also, I can explain to them, for example, what is tofu (*der-voo*, we say at home). Their mothers invite me to taste-test their Chinese cooking.

"Very authentic." I try to be reassuring. After all, they're nice people, I like them. "De-lish." I have seconds. On the question of what we eat, though, I have to admit, "Well, no, it's different than that." I have thirds. "What my mom makes is home style; it's not in the cookbooks."

Not in the cookbooks! Everyone's jealous. Meanwhile, the big deal at home is when we have turkey pot pie. My sister Callie's the one introduced them — Mrs. Wilder's, they come in this green-and-brown box — and when we have them, we both get suddenly interested in helping out in the kitchen. You know, we stand in front of the oven and help them bake. Twenty-five minutes. She and I have a deal, though, to keep it secret from school, as everybody else thinks they're gross. We think they're a big improvement over authentic Chinese home cooking. Ox-tail soup — now that's gross. Stir-fried beef with tomatoes. One day I say, "You know Ma, I have never seen a stir-fried tomato in any Chinese restaurant we have ever been in, ever."

"In China," she says, real lofty, "we consider tomatoes are a delicacy."

"Ma," I say. "Tomatoes are *Italian.*"

"No respect for elders." She wags her finger at me, but I can tell it's just to try and shame me into believing her. "I'm tell you, tomatoes *invented* in China."

"*Ma.*"

"Is true. Like noodles. Invented in China."

"That's not what they said in *school.*"

"In *China,*" my mother counters, "we also eat tomatoes uncooked, like apple. And in summertime we slice them, and put some sugar on top."

"Are you sure?"

My mom says of course she's sure, and in the end I give in, even though she once told me that China was such a long time ago, a lot of things she can hardly remember. She said sometimes she has trouble remembering her characters, that sometimes she'll be writing a letter, just writing along, and all of a sudden she won't be sure if she should put four dots or three.

"So what do you do then?"

"Oh, I just make a little sloppy."

"You mean you *fudge*?"

She laughed then, but another time, when she was showing me how to write my name, and I said, just kidding, "Are you sure that's the right number of dots now?" she was hurt.

"I mean, of course you know," I said. "I mean, *oy*."

Meanwhile, what *I* know is that in the eighth grade, what people want to hear does not include how Chinese people eat sliced tomatoes with sugar on top. For a gross fact, it just isn't gross enough. On the other hand, the fact that somewhere in China somebody eats or has eaten or once ate living monkey brains — now that's conversation.

"They have these special tables," I say, "kind of like a giant collar. With a hole in the middle, for the monkey's neck. They put the monkey in the collar, and then they cut off the top of its head."

"Whadda they use for cutting?"

I think. "Scalpels."

"*Scalpels?*" says Andy Kaplan.

"Kaplan, don't be dense," Barbara Gugelstein says. "The Chinese *invented* scalpels."

Once a friend said to me, You know, everybody is valued for something. She explained how some people resented being valued for their looks; others resented being valued for their money. Wasn't it still better to be beautiful and rich than ugly and poor, though? You should be just glad, she said, that you have something people value. It's like having a special talent, like being good at ice-skating, or opera singing. She said, You could probably make a career out of it.

Here's the irony: I am.

Anyway, I am ad-libbing my way through eighth grade, as I've described. Until one bloomy spring day, I come in late to homeroom, and to my chagrin discover there's a new kid in class.

Chinese.

So what should I do, pretend to have to go to the girls' room, like Barbara Gugelstein the day Andy Kaplan took his ID back? I sit down; I am so cool I remind myself of Paul Newman. First thing I realize, though, is that no one looking at me is thinking of Paul Newman. The notes fly:

"I think he's cute."

"Who?" I write back. (I am still at an age, understand, when I believe a person can be saved by aplomb.)

"I don't think he talks English too good. Writes it either."

"Who?"

"They might have to put him behind a grade, so don't worry."

"He has a crush on you already, you could tell as soon as you walked in, he turned kind of orangish."

I hope I'm not turning orangish as I deal with my mail. I could use a secretary. The second round starts:

"What do you mean who? Don't be weird. Didn't you *see* him??? Straight back over your right shoulder!!!!"

I have to look; what else can I do? I think of certain tips I learned in Girl Scouts about poise. I cross my ankles. I hold a pen in my hand. I sit up as though I have a crown on my head. I swivel my head slowly, repeating to myself, *I could be Miss America.*

"Miss Mona Chang."

Horror raises its hoary head.

"Notes, please."

Mrs. Mandeville's policy is to read all notes aloud.

I try to consider what Miss America would do, and see myself, back straight, knees together, crying. Some inspiration. Cool Hand Luke, on the other hand, would, quick, eat the evidence. And why not? I should yawn as I stand up, and boom, the notes are gone. All that's left is to explain that it's an old Chinese reflex.

I shuffle up to the front of the room.

"One minute please," Mrs. Mandeville says.

I wait, noticing how large and plastic her mouth is.

She unfolds a piece of paper.

And I, Miss Mona Chang, who got almost straight A's her whole life except in math and conduct, am about to start crying in front of everyone.

I am delivered out of hot Egypt by the bell. General pandemonium. Mrs. Mandeville still has her hand clamped on my shoulder, though. And the next thing I know, I'm holding the new boy's schedule. He's standing next to me like a big blank piece of paper. "This is Sherman," Mrs. Mandeville says.

"Hello," I say.

"*Non how a,*" I say.

I'm glad Barbara Gugelstein isn't there to see my Chinese in action.

"*Ji nu,*" I say. "*Shee veh.*"

Later I find out that his mother asked if there were any other Orientals in our grade. She had him put in my class on purpose. For now, though, he looks at me as though I'm much stranger than anything else he's seen so far. Is this because he understands I'm saying "soy sauce rice gruel" to him or because he doesn't?

"Sher-man," he says finally.

I look at his schedule card. Sherman Matsumoto. What kind of name is that for a nice Chinese boy?

(Later on, people ask me how I can tell Chinese from Japanese. I shrug. You just kind of know, I say. Oy!)

Sherman's got the sort of looks I think of as pretty-boy. Monsignor black hair (not monk brown like mine), bouncy. Crayola eyebrows, one with a round bald spot in the middle of it, like a golf hole. I don't know how anybody can think of him as orangish; his skin looks white to me, with pink triangles hanging down the front of his cheeks like flags. Kind of delicate-looking, but the only truly uncool thing about him is that his spiral notebook has a picture of a kitty cat on it. A big white fluffy one, with a blue ribbon above each perky little ear. I get much opportunity to view this, as all the poor kid understands about life in junior high school is that he should follow me everywhere. It's embarrassing. On the other hand, he's obviously even more miserable than I am, so I try not to say anything. Give him a chance to adjust. We communicate by sign language, and by drawing pictures, which he's better at than I am; he puts in every last detail, even if it takes forever. I try to be patient.

A week of this. Finally I enlighten him. "You should get a new notebook."

His cheeks turn a shade of pink you mostly only see in hyacinths.

"Notebook." I point to his. I show him mine, which is psychedelic, with big purple and yellow stick-on flowers. I try to explain he should have one like this, only without the flowers. He nods enigmatically, and the next day brings me a notebook just like his, except that this cat sports pink bows instead of blue.

"Pret-ty," he says. "You."

He speaks English! I'm dumbfounded. Has he spoken it all this time? I consider: Pretty. You. What does that mean? Plus actually, he's said *plit-ty*, much as my parents would; I'm assuming he means pretty, but maybe he means pity. Pity. You.

"Jeez," I say finally.

"You are wel-come," he says.

I decorate the back of the notebook with stick-on flowers, and hold it so that these show when I walk though the halls. In class I mostly keep my book open. After all, the kid's so new; I think I really ought to have a heart. And for a live-long day nobody notices.

Then Barbara Gugelstein sidles up. "Matching notebooks, huh?"

I'm speechless.

"First comes love, then comes marriage, and then come Chappies in a baby carriage."

"Barbara!"

"Get it?" she says. "Chinese Japs."

"Bar-*bra*," I say to get even.

"Just make sure he doesn't give you any *tea*," she says.

Are Sherman and I in love? Three days later, I hazard that we are. My thinking proceeds this way: I think he's cute, and I think he thinks I'm cute. On the other hand, we don't kiss and we don't exactly have fantastic conversations. Our talks *are* getting better, though. We started out, "This is a book." "Book." "This is a chair." "Chair." Advancing to, "What is this?" "This is a book." Now, for fun, he tests me.

"What is this?" he says.

"This is a book," I say, as if I'm the one who has to learn how to talk.

He claps. "Good!"

Meanwhile, people ask me all about him. I could be his press agent.

"No, he doesn't eat raw fish."

"No, his father wasn't a kamikaze pilot."

"No, he can't do karate."

"Are you sure?" somebody asks.

Indeed he doesn't know karate, but judo he does. I am hurt I'm not the one to find this out; the guys know from gym class. They line up to be flipped, he flips them all onto the floor, and after that he doesn't eat lunch at the girls' table with me anymore. I'm more or less glad. Meaning, when he was there, I never knew what to say. Now that he's gone, though, I seem to be stuck at the "This is a chair" level of conversation. Ancient Chinese eating habits have lost their cachet; all I get are more and more questions about me and Sherman. "I dunno," I'm saying all the time. *Are* we going out? We do stuff, it's true. For example, I take him to the department stores, explain to him who shops in Alexander's, who shops in Saks. I tell him my family's the type that shops in Alexander's. He says he's sorry. In Saks he gets lost; either that, or else I'm the lost one. (It's true I find him calmly waiting at the front door, hands behind his back, like a guard.) I take him to the candy store. I take him to the bagel store. Sherman is crazy about bagels. I explain to him that Lender's is gross, he should get his bagels from the bagel store. He says thank you.

"Are you going steady?" people want to know.

How can we go steady when he doesn't have an ID brace-

let? On the other hand, he brings me more presents than I
think any girl's ever gotten before. Oranges. Flowers. A little
bag of bagels. But what do they mean? Do they mean thank
you, I enjoyed our trip; do they mean I like you; do they
mean I decided I liked the Lender's better even if they are
gross, you can have these? Sometimes I think he's acting on
his mother's instructions. Also I know at least a couple of the
presents were supposed to go to our teachers. He told me that
once and turned red. I figured it still might mean something
that he didn't throw them out.

More and more now, we joke. Like, instead of "I'm thinking," he always says, "I'm sinking," which we both think is
so funny, that all either one of us has to do is pretend to be
drowning and the other one cracks up. And he tells me things
— for example, that there are electric lights everywhere in
Tokyo now.

"You mean you didn't have them before?"

"Everywhere now!" He's amazed too. "Since Olympics!"

"Olympics?"

"Nineteen-sixty," he says proudly, and as proof, hums for
me the Olympic theme song. "You know?"

"Sure," I say, and hum with him happily. We could be a
picture on a UNICEF poster. The only problem is that I don't
really understand what the Olympics have to do with the
modernization of Japan, any more than I get this other story
he tells me, about that hole in his left eyebrow, which is from
some time his father accidentally hit him with a lit cigarette.
When Sherman was a baby. His father was drunk, having
been out carousing; his mother was very mad but didn't say
anything, just cleaned the whole house. Then his father was
so ashamed he bowed to ask her forgiveness.

"Your mother cleaned the house?"

Sherman nods solemnly.

"And your father *bowed?*" I find this more astounding than anything I ever thought to make up. "That is so weird," I tell him.

"Weird," he agrees. "This I no forget, forever. *Father* bow to *mother!*"

We shake our heads.

As for the things he asks me, they're not topics I ever discussed before. Do I like it here? Of course I like it here, I was born here, I say. Am I Jewish? Jewish! I laugh. Oy! Am I American? "Sure I'm American," I say. "Everybody who's born here is American, and also some people who convert from what they were before. You could become American." But he says no, he could never. "Sure you could," I say. "You only have to learn some rules and speeches."

"But I Japanese," he says.

"You could become American anyway," I say. "Like I *could* become Jewish, if I wanted to. I'd just have to switch, that's all."

"But you Catholic," he says.

I think maybe he doesn't get what means switch.

I introduce him to Mrs. Wilder's turkey pot pies. "Gross?" he asks. I say they are, but we like them anyway. "Don't tell anybody." He promises. We bake them, eat them. While we're eating, he's drawing me pictures.

"This American," he says, and he draws something that looks like John Wayne. "This Jewish," he says, and draws something that looks like the Wicked Witch of the West, only male.

"I don't think so," I say.

He's undeterred. "This Japanese," he says, and draws a fair rendition of himself. "This Chinese," he says, and draws what looks to be another fair rendition of himself.

"How can you tell them apart?"

"This way," he says, and he puts the picture of the Chinese so that it is looking at the pictures of the American and the Jew. The Japanese faces the wall. Then he draws another picture, of a Japanese flag, so that the Japanese has that to contemplate. "Chinese lost in department store," he says. "Japanese know how go." For fun, he then takes the Japanese flag and fastens it to the refrigerator door with magnets. "In school, in ceremony, we this way," he explains, and bows to the picture.

When my mother comes in, her face is so red that with the white wall behind her she looks a bit like the Japanese flag herself. Yet I get the feeling I better not say so. First she doesn't move. Then she snatches the flag off the refrigerator, so fast the magnets go flying. Two of them land on the stove. She crumples up the paper. She hisses at Sherman, *"This is the U.S. of A., do you hear me!"*

Sherman hears her.

"You call your mother right now. Tell her come pick you up."

He understands perfectly. *I*, on the other hand, am stymied. How can two people who don't really speak English understand each other better than I can understand them? "But Ma," I say.

"Don't *Ma* me," she says.

Later on she explains that World War II was in China too. "Hitler," I say. "Nazis. Volkswagens." I know the Japanese were on the wrong side, because they bombed Pearl Harbor. My mother explains about before that. The Napkin Massacre. *"Nan*-king," she corrects me.

"Are you sure?" I say. "In school, they said the war was about putting the Jews in ovens."

"Also about ovens."

"About both?"

"Both."

"That's not what they said in school."

"Just forget about school."

Forget about school? "I thought we moved here for the schools."

"We moved here," she says, "for your education."

Sometimes I have no idea what she's talking about.

"I like Sherman," I say after a while.

"He's nice boy," she agrees.

Meaning what? I would ask, except that my dad's just come home, which means it's time to start talking about whether we should build a brick wall across the front of the lawn. Recently a car made it almost into our livingroom, which was so scary, the driver fainted and an ambulance had to come. "We should have discussion," my dad said after that. And so for about a week, every night we do.

"Are you just friends, or more than just friends?" Barbara Gugelstein is giving me the cross-ex.

"Maybe," I say.

"Come on," she says, "I told you *everything* about me and Andy."

I actually *am* trying to tell Barbara everything about Sherman, but everything turns out to be nothing. Meaning, I can't locate the conversation in what I have to say. Sherman and I go places, we talk, one time my mother threw him out of the house because of World War II.

"I think we're just friends," I say.

"You think or you're sure?"

Now that I do less of the talking at lunch, I notice more what other people talk about — cheerleading, who likes who, this place in White Plains to get earrings. On none of these topics am I an expert. Of course, I'm still friends with Barbara Gugelstein, but I notice Danielle Meyers has spun away to other groups.

Barbara's analysis goes this way: To be popular, you have to have big boobs, a note from your mother that lets you use her Lord and Taylor credit card, and a boyfriend. On the other hand, what's so wrong with being unpopular? "We'll get them in the end," she says. It's what her dad tells her. "Like they'll turn out too dumb to do their own investing, and then they'll get killed in fees and then they'll have to move to towns where the schools stink. And my dad should know," she winds up. "He's a broker."

"I guess," I say.

But the next thing I know, I have a true crush on Sherman Matsumoto. Mister Judo, the guys call him now, with real respect; and the more they call him that, the more I don't care that he carries a notebook with a cat on it.

I sigh. "Sherman."

"I thought you were just friends," says Barbara Gugelstein.

"We were," I say mysteriously. This, I've noticed, is how Danielle Meyers talks; everything's secret, she only lets out so much, it's like she didn't grow up with everybody telling her she had to share.

And here's the funny thing: The more I intimate that Sherman and I are more than just friends, the more it seems we actually are. It's the old imagination giving reality a nudge. When I start to blush, he starts to blush; we reach a point where we can hardly talk at all.

"Well, there's first base with tongue, and first base without," I tell Barbara Gugelstein.

In fact, Sherman and I have brushed shoulders, which was equivalent to first base I was sure, maybe even second. I felt as though I'd turned into one huge shoulder; that's all I was, one huge shoulder. We not only didn't talk, we didn't breathe. But how can I tell Barbara Gugelstein that? So instead I say, "Well there's second base and second base."

Danielle Meyers is my friend again. She says, "I know exactly what you mean," just to make Barbara Gugelstein feel bad.

"Like *what* do I mean?" I say.

Danielle Meyers can't answer.

"You know what I think?" I tell Barbara the next day. "I think Danielle's giving us a line."

Barbara pulls thoughtfully on one of her pigtails.

If Sherman Matsumoto is never going to give me an ID to wear, he should at least get up the nerve to hold my hand. I don't think he sees this. I think of the story he told me about his parents, and in a synaptic firestorm realize we don't see the same things at all.

So one day, when we happen to brush shoulders again, I don't move away. He doesn't move away either. There we are. Like a pair of bleachers, pushed together but not quite matched up. After a while, I have to breathe, I can't help it. I breathe in such a way that our elbows start to touch too. We are in a crowd, waiting for a bus. I crane my neck to look at the sign that says where the bus is going; now our wrists are touching. Then it happens: He links his pinky around mine.

Is that holding hands? Later, in bed, I wonder all night. One finger, and not even the biggest one.

Sherman is leaving in a month. Already! I think, well, I suppose he will leave and we'll never even kiss. I guess that's all right. Just when I've resigned myself to it, though, we hold hands all five fingers. Once when we are at the bagel shop, then again in my parents' kitchen. Then, when we are at the playground, he kisses the back of my hand.

He does it again not too long after that, in White Plains.

I invest in a bottle of mouthwash.

Instead of moving on, though, he kisses the back of my hand again. And again. I try raising my hand, hoping he'll make the jump from my hand to my cheek. It's like trying to wheedle an inchworm out the window. You know, *This way, this way.*

All over the world, people have their own cultures. That's what we learned in social studies.

If we never kiss, I'm not going to take it personally.

It is the end of the school year. We've had parties. We've turned in our textbooks. Hooray! Outside the asphalt already steams if you spit on it. Sherman isn't leaving for another couple of days, though, and he comes to visit every morning, staying until the afternoon, when Callie comes home from her big-deal job as a bank teller. We drink Kool-Aid in the backyard and hold hands until they are sweaty and make smacking noises coming apart. He tells me how busy his parents are, getting ready for the move. His mother, particularly, is very tired. Mostly we are mournful.

The very last day we hold hands and do not let go. Our palms fill up with water like a blister. We do not care. We talk more than usual. How much airmail is to Japan, that kind of thing. Then suddenly he asks, will I marry him?

I'm only thirteen.

But when old? Sixteen?

If you come back to get me.

I come. Or you can come to Japan, be Japanese.

How can I be Japanese?

Like you become American. Switch.

He kisses me on the cheek, again and again and again.

His mother calls to say she's coming to get him. I cry. I tell him how I've saved every present he's ever given me — the ruler, the pencils, the bags from the bagels, all the flower petals. I even have the orange peels from the oranges.

All?

I put them in a jar.

I'd show him, except that we're not allowed to go upstairs to my room. Anyway, something about the orange peels seems to choke him up too. Mister Judo, but I've gotten him in a soft spot. We are going together to the bathroom to get some toilet paper to wipe our eyes when poor tired Mrs. Matsumoto, driving a shiny new station wagon, skids up onto our lawn.

"Very sorry!"

We race outside.

"Very sorry!"

Mrs. Matsumoto is so short that about all we can see of her is a green cotton sun hat, with a big brim. It's tied on. The brim is trembling.

I hope my mom's not going to start yelling about World War II.

"Is all right, no trouble," she says, materializing on the steps behind me and Sherman. She's propped the screen door wide open; when I turn I see she's waving. "No trouble, no trouble!"

"No trouble, no trouble!" I echo, twirling a few times with relief.

Mrs. Matsumoto keeps apologizing; my mom keeps insisting she shouldn't feel bad, it was only some grass and a small

tree. Crossing the lawn, she insists Mrs. Matsumoto get out
of the car, even though it means trampling some lilies of the
valley. She insists that Mrs. Matsumoto come in for a cup
of tea. Then she will not talk about anything unless Mrs.
Matsumoto sits down, and unless she lets my mom prepare
her a small snack. The coming in and the tea and the sitting
down are settled pretty quickly, but they negotiate ferociously
over the small snack, which Mrs. Matsumoto will not eat
unless she can call Mr. Matsumoto. She makes the mistake
of linking Mr. Matsumoto with a reparation of some sort,
which my mom will not hear of.

"Please!"

"No no no no."

Back and forth it goes: "No no no no." "No no no no."
"No no no no." What kind of conversation is that? I look at
Sherman, who shrugs. Finally Mr. Matsumoto calls on his
own, wondering where his wife is. He comes over in a taxi.
He's a heavy-browed businessman, friendly but brisk — not
at all a type you could imagine bowing to a lady with a taste
for tie-on sunhats. My mom invites him in as if it's an idea
she just this moment thought of. And would he maybe have
some tea and a small snack?

Sherman and I sneak back outside for another farewell, by
the side of the house, behind the forsythia bushes. We hold
hands. He kisses me on the cheek again, and then — just
when I think he's finally going to kiss me on the lips — he
kisses me on the neck.

Is this first base?

He does it more. Up and down, up and down. First it
tickles, and then it doesn't. He has his eyes closed. I close
my eyes too. He's hugging me. Up and down. Then down.

He's at my collarbone.

Still at my collarbone. Now his hand's on my ribs. So

much for first base. More ribs. The idea of second base would probably make me nervous if he weren't on his way back to Japan and if I really thought we were going to get there. As it is, though, I'm not in much danger of wrecking my life on the shoals of passion; his unmoving hand feels more like a growth than a boyfriend. He has his whole face pressed to my neck skin so I can't tell his mouth from his nose. I think he may be licking me.

From indoors, a burst of adult laughter. My eyelids flutter. I start to try and wiggle such that his hand will maybe budge upward.

Do I mean for my top blouse button to come accidentally undone?

He clenches his jaw, and when he opens his eyes, they're fixed on that button like it's a gnat that's been bothering him for far too long. He mutters in Japanese. If later in life he were to describe this as a pivotal moment in his youth, I would not be surprised. Holding the material as far from my body as possible, he buttons the button. Somehow we've landed up too close to the bushes.

What to tell Barbara Gugelstein? She says, "Tell me what were his last words. He must have said something last."

"I don't want to talk about it."

"Maybe he said, Good-bye?" she suggests. "*Sayonara?*" She means well.

"I don't want to talk about it."

"Aw, come on, I told you everything about . . ."

I say, "Because it's private, excuse me."

She stops, squints at me as though at a far-off face she's trying to make out. Then she nods and very lightly places her hand on my forearm.

*   *   *

The forsythia seemed to be stabbing us in the eyes. Sherman said, more or less, *You will need to study how to switch.*

And I said, *I think you should switch. The way you do everything is weird.*

And he said, *You just want to tell everything to your friends. You just want to have boyfriend to become popular.*

Then he flipped me. Two swift moves, and I went sprawling through the air, a flailing confusion of soft human parts such as had no idea where the ground was.

It is the fall, and I am in high school, and still he hasn't written, so finally I write him.

I still have all your gifts, I write. *I don't talk so much as I used to. Although I am not exactly a mouse either. I don't care about being popular anymore. I swear. Are you happy to be back in Japan? I know I ruined everything. I was just trying to be entertaining. I miss you with all my heart, and hope I didn't ruin everything.*

He writes back, *You will never be Japanese.*

I throw all the orange peels out that day. Some of them, it turns out, were moldy anyway. I tell my mother I want to move to Chinatown.

"Chinatown!" she says.

I don't know why I suggested it.

"What's the matter?" she says. "Still boy-crazy? That Sherman?"

"No."

"Too much homework?"

I don't answer.

"Forget about school."

Later she tells me if I don't like school, I don't have to go every day. Some days I can stay home.

"Stay home?" In Yonkers, Callie and I used to stay home

all the time, but that was because the schools there were a *waste of time.*

"No good for a girl to be too smart anyway."

For a long time I think about Sherman. But after a while I don't think about him so much as I just keep seeing myself flipped onto the ground, lying there shocked as the Matsumotos get ready to leave. My head has hit a rock; my brain aches as though it's been shoved to some new place in my skull. Otherwise I am okay. I see the forsythia, all those whippy branches, and can't believe how many leaves there are on a bush — every one green and perky and durably itself. And past them, real sky. I try to remember about why the sky's blue, even though this one's gone the kind of indescribable gray you associate with the insides of old shoes. I smell grass. Probably I have grass stains all over my back. I hear my mother calling through the back door, "Mon-a! Everyone leaving now," and "Not coming to say good-bye?" I hear Mr. and Mrs. Matsumoto bowing as they leave — or at least I hear the embarrassment in my mother's voice as they bow. I hear their car start. I hear Mrs. Matsumoto directing Mr. Matsumoto how to back off the lawn so as not to rip any more of it up. I feel the back of my head for blood — just a little. I hear their *chug-chug* grow fainter and fainter, until it has faded into the *whuzz-whuzz* of all the other cars. I hear my mom singing, "Mon-a! Mon-a!" until my dad comes home. Doors open and shut. I see myself standing up, brushing myself off so I'll have less explaining to do if she comes out to look for me. Grass stains — just like I thought. I see myself walking around the house, going over to have a look at our churned-up yard. It looks pretty sad, two big brown tracks, right through the irises and the lilies of the valley, and that was a new dogwood we'd just planted. Lying there like that. I hear myself thinking about my father, having to go dig it up all over again. Adjusting. I think how we probably ought to put up that brick wall. And sure enough, when I go inside, no one's thinking about me, or that little bit of blood at the back of my head, or the grass stains. That's what they're talking about — that wall. Again. My mom doesn't think it'll do any good, but my dad thinks we should give it a try. Should we or shouldn't we? How high? How thick? What will the neighbors say? I plop myself down on a hard chair. And all I can think is, we are the complete only family that has to worry about this. If I could, I'd switch everything to be different. But since I can't, I might as well sit here at the table for a while, discussing what I know how to discuss. I nod and listen to the rest.

My Lucy Friend Who Smells Like Corn

Sandra Cisneros

Lucy Anguiano, Texas girl who smells like corn, like Frito
Bandito chips, like tortillas, something like that warm smell
of *nixtamal* or bread the way her head smells when she's leaning close to you over a paper cut-out doll or on the porch
when we are squatting over marbles trading this pretty crystal
that leaves a blue star on your hand for that giant cat-eye
with a grasshopper green spiral in the center like the juice of
bugs on the windshield when you drive to the border, like
the yellow blood of butterflies.

Have you ever eated dog food? I have. After crunching like
ice, she opens her big mouth to prove it, only a pink tongue
rolling around in there like a blind worm, and Janey looking
in because she said Show me. But me I like that Lucy, corn
smell hair and aqua flip-flops just like mine that we bought
at the K mart for only 79 cents same time.

I'm going to sit in the sun, don't care if it's a million trillion
degrees outside, so my skin can get so dark it's blue where it
bends like Lucy's. Her whole family like that. Eyes like knife
slits. Lucy and her sisters. Norma, Margarita, Ofelia, Her-
minia, Nancy, Olivia, Cheli, *y la* Amber Sue.

Screen door with no screen. *Bang!* Little black dog biting his fur. Fat couch on the porch. Some of the windows painted blue, some pink, because her daddy got tired that day or forgot. Mama in the kitchen feeding clothes into the wringer washer and clothes rolling out all stiff and twisted and flat like paper. Lucy got her arm stuck once and had to yell Maaa! and her mama had to put the machine in reverse and then her hand rolled back, the finger black and later, her nail fell off. *But did your arm get flat like the clothes? What happened to your arm? Did they have to pump it with air?* No, only the finger, and she didn't cry neither.

Lean across the porch rail and pin the pink sock of the baby Amber Sue on top of Cheli's flowered T-shirt, and the blue jeans of *la* Ofelia over the inside seam of Olivia's blouse, over the flannel nightgown of Margarita so it don't stretch out, and then you take the work shirts of their daddy and hang them upside down like this, and this way all the clothes don't get so wrinkled and take up less space and you don't waste pins. The girls all wear each other's clothes, except Olivia, who is stingy. There ain't no boys here. Only girls and one father who is never home hardly and one mother who says *Ay! I'm real tired* and so many sisters there's no time to count them.

I'm sitting in the sun even though it's the hottest part of the day, the part that makes the streets dizzy, when the heat makes a little hat on the top of your head and bakes the dust and weed grass and sweat up good, all steamy and smelling like sweet corn.

I want to rub heads and sleep in a bed with little sisters, some at the top and some at the feets. I think it would be fun to sleep with sisters you could yell at one at a time or all together, instead of alone on the fold-out chair in the living room.

When I get home Abuelita will say *Didn't I tell you?* and I'll get it because I was supposed to wear this dress again tomorrow. But first I'm going to jump off an old pissy mattress in the Anguiano yard. I'm going to scratch your mosquito bites, Lucy, so they'll itch you, then put Mercurochrome smiley faces on them. We're going to trade shoes and wear them on our hands. We're going to walk over to Janey Ortiz's house and say *We're never ever going to be your friend again forever!* We're going to run home backwards and we're going to run home frontwards, look twice under the house where the rats hide and I'll stick one foot in there because you dared me, sky so blue and heaven inside those white clouds. I'm going to peel a scab from my knee and eat it, sneeze on the cat, give you three M & M's I've been saving for you since yesterday, comb your hair with my fingers and braid it into teeny-tiny braids real pretty. We're going to wave to a lady we don't know on the bus. Hello! I'm going to somersault on the rail of the front porch even though my *chones* show. And cut paper dolls we draw ourselves, and color in their clothes with crayons, my arm around your neck.

And when we look at each other, our arms gummy from an orange Popsicle we split, we could be sisters, right? We could be, you and me waiting for our teeths to fall and money. You laughing something into my ear that tickles, and me going Ha Ha Ha Ha. Her and me, my Lucy friend who smells like corn.

Sucker

Carson McCullers

It was always like I had a room to myself. Sucker slept in my bed with me but that didn't interfere with anything. The room was mine and I used it as I wanted to. Once I remember sawing a trap door in the floor. Last year when I was a sophomore in high school I tacked on my wall some pictures of girls from magazines and one of them was just in her underwear. My mother never bothered me because she had the younger kids to look after. And Sucker thought anything I did was always swell.

Whenever I would bring any of my friends back to my room all I had to do was just glance once at Sucker and he would get up from whatever he was busy with and maybe half smile at me, and leave without saying a word. He never brought kids back there. He's twelve, four years younger than I am, and he always knew without me even telling him that I didn't want kids that age meddling with my things.

Half the time I used to forget that Sucker isn't my brother. He's my first cousin but practically ever since I remember he's been in our family. You see his folks were killed in a wreck when he was a baby. To me and my kid sisters he was like our brother.

Sucker used to always remember and believe every word I said. That's how he got his nickname. Once a couple of years ago I told him that if he'd jump off our garage with an umbrella it would act as a parachute and he wouldn't fall hard. He did it and busted his knee. That's just one instance. And the funny thing was that no matter how many times he got fooled he would still believe me. Not that he was dumb in other ways — it was just the way he acted with me. He would look at everything I did and quietly take it in.

There is one thing I have learned, but it makes me feel guilty and is hard to figure out. If a person admires you a lot you despise him and don't care — and it is the person who doesn't notice you that you are apt to admire. This is not easy to realize. Maybelle Watts, this senior at school, acted like she was the Queen of Sheba and even humiliated me. Yet at this same time I would have done anything in the world to get her attentions. All I could think about day and night was Maybelle until I was nearly crazy. When Sucker was a little kid and on up until the time he was twelve I guess I treated him as bad as Maybelle did me.

Now that Sucker has changed so much it is a little hard to remember him as he used to be. I never imagined anything would suddenly happen that would make us both very different. I never knew that in order to get what has happened straight in my mind I would want to think back on him as he used to be and compare and try to get things settled. If I could have seen ahead maybe I would have acted different.

I never noticed him much or thought about him and when you consider how long we have had the same room together it is funny the few things I remember. He used to talk to himself a lot when he'd think he was alone — all about him fighting gangsters and being on ranches and that sort of kids' stuff. He'd get in the bathroom and stay as long as an hour and sometimes his voice would go up high and excited and you could hear him all over the house. Usually, though, he was very quiet. He didn't have many boys in the neighborhood to buddy with and his face had the look of a kid who is watching a game and waiting to be asked to play. He didn't mind wearing the sweaters and coats that I outgrew, even if the sleeves did flop down too big and make his wrists look as thin and white as a little girl's. That is how I remember him — getting a little bigger every year but still being the same. That was Sucker up until a few months ago when all this trouble began.

Maybelle was somehow mixed up in what happened so I guess I ought to start with her. Until I knew her I hadn't given much time to girls. Last fall she sat next to me in General Science class and that was when I first began to notice her. Her hair is the brightest yellow I ever saw and occasionally she will wear it set into curls with some sort of gluey stuff. Her fingernails are pointed and manicured and painted a shiny red. All during class I used to watch Maybelle, nearly all the time except when I thought she was going to look my way or when the teacher called on me. I couldn't keep my eyes off her hands, for one thing. They are very little and white except for that red stuff, and when she would turn the pages of her book she always licked her thumb and held out her little finger and turned very slowly. It is impossible to describe Maybelle. All the boys are crazy about her but she didn't even notice me. For one thing she's almost two years older than I am. Between periods I used to try and pass very close to her in the halls but she would hardly ever smile at me. All I could do was sit and look at her in class — and sometimes it was like the whole room could hear my heart beating and I wanted to holler or light out and run for Hell.

At night, in bed, I would imagine about Maybelle. Often

this would keep me from sleeping until as late as one or two o'clock. Sometimes Sucker would wake up and ask me why I couldn't get settled and I'd tell him to hush his mouth. I suppose I was mean to him lots of times. I guess I wanted to ignore somebody like Maybelle did me. You could always tell by Sucker's face when his feelings were hurt. I don't remember all the ugly remarks I must have made because even when I was saying them my mind was on Maybelle.

That went on for nearly three months and then somehow she began to change. In the halls she would speak to me and every morning she copied my homework. At lunchtime once I danced with her in the gym. One afternoon I got up nerve and went around to her house with a carton of cigarettes. I knew she smoked in the girls' basement and sometimes outside of school — and I didn't want to take her candy because I think that's been run into the ground. She was very nice and it seemed to me everything was going to change.

It was that night when this trouble really started. I had come into my room late and Sucker was already asleep. I felt too happy and keyed up to get in a comfortable position and I was awake thinking about Maybelle a long time. Then I dreamed about her and it seemed I kissed her. It was a surprise to wake up and see that dark. I lay still and a little while passed before I could come to and understand where I was. The house was quiet and it was a very dark night.

Sucker's voice was a shock to me. "Pete . . . ?"

I didn't answer anything or even move.

"You do like me as much as if I was your own brother, don't you, Pete?"

I couldn't get over the surprise of everything and it was like this was the real dream instead of the other.

"You have liked me all the time like I was your own brother, haven't you?"

"Sure," I said.

Then I got up for a few minutes. It was cold and I was glad to come back to bed. Sucker hung on to my back. He felt little and warm and I could feel his warm breathing on my shoulder.

"No matter what you did I always knew you liked me."

I was wide awake and my mind seemed mixed up in a strange way. There was this happiness about Maybelle and all that — but at the same time something about Sucker and his voice when he said these things made me take notice. Anyway I guess you understand people better when you are happy than when something is worrying you. It was like I had never really thought about Sucker until then. I felt I had always been mean to him. One night a few weeks before I had heard him crying in the dark. He said he had lost a boy's beebee gun and was scared to let anybody know. He wanted me to tell him what to do. I was sleepy and tried to make him hush and when he wouldn't I kicked at him. That was just one of the things I remembered. It seemed to me he had always been a lonesome kid. I felt bad.

There is something about a dark cold night that makes you feel close to someone you're sleeping with. When you talk together it is like you are the only people awake in the town.

"You're a swell kid, Sucker," I said.

It seemed to me suddenly that I did like him more than anybody else I knew — more than any other boy, more than my sisters, more in a certain way even than Maybelle. I felt good all over and it was like when they play sad music in the movies. I wanted to show Sucker how much I really thought of him and make up for the way I had always treated him.

We talked for a good while that night. His voice was fast and it was like he had been saving up these things to tell me for a long time. He mentioned that he was going to try to build a canoe and that the kids down the block wouldn't let him in on their football team and I don't know what all. I talked some too and it was a good feeling to think of him taking in everything I said so seriously. I even spoke of Maybelle a little, only I made out like it was her who had been running after me all this time. He asked questions about high school and so forth. His voice was excited and he kept on talking fast like he could never get the words out in time. When I went to sleep he was still talking and I could still feel his breathing on my shoulder, warm and close.

During the next couple of weeks I saw a lot of Maybelle. She acted as though she really cared for me a little. Half the time I felt so good I hardly knew what to do with myself.

But I didn't forget about Sucker. There were a lot of old things in my bureau drawer I'd been saving — boxing gloves and Tom Swift books and second rate fishing tackle. All this I turned over to him. We had some more talks together and it was really like I was knowing him for the first time. When there was a long cut on his cheek I knew he had been monkeying around with this new first razor set of mine, but I didn't say anything. His face seemed different now. He used to look timid and sort of like he was afraid of a whack over the head. That expression was gone. His face, with those wide-open eyes and his ears sticking out and his mouth never quite shut, had the look of a person who is surprised and expecting something swell.

Once I started to point him out to Maybelle and tell her he was my kid brother. It was an afternoon when a murder mystery was on at the movie. I had earned a dollar working for my Dad and I gave Sucker a quarter to go and get candy and so forth. With the rest I took Maybelle. We were sitting near the back and I saw Sucker come in. He began to stare at the screen the minute he stepped past the ticket man and he stumbled down the aisle without noticing where he was going. I started to punch Maybelle but couldn't quite make up my mind. Sucker looked a little silly — walking like a drunk with his eyes glued to the movie. He was wiping his reading glasses on his shirt tail and his knickers flopped down. He went on until he got to the first few rows where the kids usually sit. I never did punch Maybelle. But I got to thinking it was good to have both of them at the movie with the money I earned.

I guess things went on like this for about a month or six weeks. I felt so good I couldn't settle down to study or put my mind on anything. I wanted to be friendly with everybody. There were times when I just had to talk to some person. And usually that would be Sucker. He felt as good as I did. Once he said: "Pete, I am gladder that you are like my brother than anything else in the world."

Then something happened between Maybelle and me. I never have figured out just what it was. Girls like her are hard to understand. She began to act different toward me. At first I wouldn't let myself believe this and tried to think it was just my imagination. She didn't act glad to see me anymore. Often she went out riding with this fellow on the football team who owns this yellow roadster. The car was the color of her hair and after school she would ride off with him, laughing and looking into his face. I couldn't think of anything to do about it and she was on my mind all day and night. When I did get a chance to go out with her she was snippy and didn't seem to notice me. This made me feel like something was the matter — I would worry about my shoes clopping too loud on the floor or the fly of my pants, or the bumps on my chin. Sometimes when Maybelle was around, a devil would get into me and I'd hold my face stiff and call grown men by their last names without the Mister and say rough things. In the night

I would wonder what made me do all this until I was too tired for sleep.

At first I was so worried I just forgot about Sucker. Then later he began to get on my nerves. He was always hanging around until I would get back from high school, always looking like he had something to say to me or wanted me to tell him. He made me a magazine rack in his Manual Training class and one week he saved his lunch money and bought me three packs of cigarettes. He couldn't seem to take it in that I had things on my mind and didn't want to fool with him. Every afternoon it would be the same — him in my room with this waiting expression on his face. Then I wouldn't say anything or I'd maybe answer him rough-like and he would finally go on out.

I can't divide that time up and say this happened one day and that the next. For one thing I was so mixed up the weeks just slid along into each other and I felt like Hell and didn't care. Nothing definite was said or done. Maybelle still rode around with this fellow in his yellow roadster and sometimes she would smile at me and sometimes not. Every afternoon I went from one place to another where I thought she would be. Either she would act almost nice and I would begin thinking how things would finally clear up and she would care for me — or else she'd behave so that if she hadn't been a girl I'd have wanted to grab her by that white little neck and choke her. The more ashamed I felt for making a fool of myself the more I ran after her.

Sucker kept getting on my nerves more and more. He would look at me as though he sort of blamed me for something, but at the same time knew that it wouldn't last long. He was growing fast and for some reason began to stutter when he talked. Sometimes he had nightmares or would throw up his breakfast. Mom got him a bottle of cod liver oil.

Then the finish came between Maybelle and me. I met her going to the drugstore and asked for a date. When she said no I remarked something sarcastic. She told me she was sick and tired of my being around and that she had never cared a rap about me. She said all that. I just stood there and didn't answer anything. I walked home very slowly.

For several afternoons I stayed in my room by myself. I didn't want to go anywhere or talk to anyone. When Sucker would come in and look at me sort of funny I'd yell at him to get out. I didn't want to think of Maybelle and I sat at my desk reading *Popular Mechanics* or whittling at a toothbrush rack I was making. It seemed to me I was putting that girl out of my mind pretty well.

But you can't help what happens to you at night. That is what made things how they are now.

You see a few nights after Maybelle said those words to me I dreamed about her again. It was like that first time and I was squeezing Sucker's arm so tight I woke him up. He reached for my hand.

"Pete, what's the matter with you?"

All of a sudden I felt so mad my throat choked — at myself and the dream and Maybelle and Sucker and every single person I knew. I remembered all the times Maybelle had humiliated me and everything bad that had ever happened. It seemed to me for a second that nobody would ever like me but a sap like Sucker.

"Why is it we aren't buddies like we were before? Why — ?"

"Shut your damn trap!" I threw off the cover and got up and turned on the light. He sat in the middle of the bed, his eyes blinking and scared.

There was something in me and I couldn't help myself. I don't think anybody ever gets that mad but once. Words came without me knowing what they would be. It was only afterward that I could remember each thing I said and see it all in a clear way.

"Why aren't we buddies? Because you're the dumbest slob I ever saw! Nobody cares anything about you! And just because I felt sorry for you sometimes and tried to act decent don't think I give a damn about a dumb-bunny like you!"

If I'd talked loud or hit him it wouldn't have been so bad. But my voice was slow and like I was very calm. Sucker's mouth was partway open and he looked as though he'd knocked his funny bone. His face was white and sweat came out on his forehead. He wiped it away with the back of his hand and for a minute his arm stayed raised that way as though he was holding something away from him.

"Don't you know a single thing? Haven't you ever been around at all? Why don't you get a girlfriend instead of me? What kind of a sissy do you want to grow up to be anyway?"

I didn't know what was coming next. I couldn't help myself or think.

Sucker didn't move. He had on one of my pajama jackets and his neck stuck out skinny and small. His hair was damp on his forehead.

"Why do you always hang around me? Don't you know when you're not wanted?"

Afterward I could remember the change in Sucker's face. Slowly that blank look went away and he closed his mouth. His eyes got narrow and his fists shut. There had never been such a look on him before. It was like every second he was getting older. There was a hard look to his eyes you don't see usually in a kid. A drop of sweat rolled down his chin and he didn't notice. He just sat there with those eyes on me and he didn't speak and his face was hard and didn't move.

"No you don't know when you're not wanted. You're too dumb. Just like your name — a dumb Sucker."

It was like something had busted inside me. I turned off the light and sat down in the chair by the window. My legs were shaking and I was so tired I could have bawled. The room was cold and dark. I sat there for a long time and smoked a squashed cigarette I had saved. Outside the yard was black and quiet. After a while I heard Sucker lie down.

I wasn't mad anymore, only tired. It seemed awful to me that I had talked like that to a kid only twelve. I couldn't take it all in. I told myself I would go over to him and try to make it up. But I just sat there in the cold until a long time had passed. I planned how I could straighten it out in the morning. Then, trying not to squeak the springs, I got back in bed.

Sucker was gone when I woke up the next day. And later when I wanted to apologize as I had planned he looked at me in this new hard way so that I couldn't say a word.

All of that was two or three months ago. Since then Sucker has grown faster than any boy I ever saw. He's almost as tall as I am and his bones have gotten heavier and bigger. He won't wear any of my old clothes anymore and has bought his first pair of long pants — with some leather suspenders to hold them up. Those are just the changes that are easy to see and put into words.

Our room isn't mine at all anymore. He's gotten up this gang of kids and they have a club. When they aren't digging trenches in some vacant lot and fighting they are always in my room. On the door there is some foolishness written in Mercurochrome saying "Woe to the Outsider who Enters" and signed with crossed bones and their secret initials. They have rigged up a radio and every afternoon it blares out music. Once as I was coming in I heard a boy telling something in a loud voice about what he saw in the back of his big brother's automobile. I could guess what I didn't hear. *That's what her and my brother do. It's the truth — parked in the car.* For a minute Sucker looked surprised and his face was almost like it used to be. Then he got hard and tough again. "Sure, dumbbell. We know all that." They didn't notice me. Sucker began telling them how in two years he was planning to be a trapper in Alaska.

But most of the time Sucker stays by himself. It is worse when we are alone together in the room. He sprawls across the bed in those long curduroy pants with the suspenders and just stares at me with that hard, half-sneering look. I fiddle around my desk and can't get settled because of those eyes of his. And the thing is I just have to study because I've gotten three bad cards this term already. If I flunk English I can't graduate next year. I don't want to be a bum and I just have to get my mind on it. I don't care a flip for Maybelle or any particular girl anymore and it's only this thing between Sucker and me that is the trouble now. We never speak except when we have to before the family. I don't even want to call him Sucker anymore and unless I forget I call him by his real name, Richard. At night I can't study with him in the room and I have to hang around the drugstore, smoking and doing nothing, with the fellows who loaf there.

More than anything I want to be easy in my mind again. And I miss the way Sucker and I were for a while in a funny, sad way that before this I never would have believed. But everything is so different that there seems to be nothing I can do to get it right. I've sometimes thought if we could have it out in a big fight that would help. But I can't fight him because he's four years younger. And another thing — sometimes this look in his eyes makes me almost believe that if Sucker could he would kill me.

The Red Convertible

Louise Erdrich

for Earl Livermore

I was the first one to drive a convertible on my reservation. And of course it was red, a red Olds. I owned that car along with my brother Stephan. We owned it together until his boots filled with water on a windy night and he bought out my share. Now Stephan owns the whole car and his younger brother Marty (that's myself) walks everywhere he goes.

How did I earn enough money to buy my share in the first place? My one talent was I could always make money. I had a touch for it, unusual in a Chippewa and especially in my family. From the first I was different that way and everyone recognized it. I was the only kid they let in the Rolla legion hall to shine shoes, for example, and one Christmas I sold spiritual bouquets for the Mission door-to-door. The nuns let me keep a percentage. Once I started, it seemed the more money I made the easier the money came. Everyone encouraged it. When I was fifteen I got a job washing dishes at the Joliet Cafe, and that was where my first big break came.

It wasn't long before I was promoted to bussing tables, and then the short order cook quit and I was hired to take her place. No sooner than you know it I was managing the Joliet. The rest is history. I went on managing. I soon became part-owner and of course there was no stopping me then. It wasn't long before the whole thing was mine.

After I'd owned the Joliet one year it burned down. The whole operation. I was only twenty. I had it all and I lost it quick, but before I lost it I had every one of my relatives, and their relatives, to dinner and I also bought that red Olds I mentioned, along with Stephan.

That time we first saw it! I'll tell you when we first saw it. We had gotten a ride up to Winnepeg and both of us had money. Don't ask me why because we never mentioned a car or anything, we just had all our money. Mine was cash, a big bankroll. Stephan had two checks — a week's extra pay for being laid off, and his regular check from the Jewel Bearing Plant.

We were walking down Portage anyway, seeing the sights, when we saw it. There it was, parked, large as alive. Really as *if* it was alive. I thought of the word *repose* because the car wasn't simply stopped, parked, or whatever. That car reposed, calm and gleaming, a for sale sign in its left front window. Then before we had thought it over at all, the car belonged to us and our pockets were empty. We had just enough money for gas back home.

We went places in that car, me and Stephan. A little bit of insurance money came through from the fire and we took off driving all one whole summer. I can't tell you all the places we went to. We started off toward the Little Knife River and Mandaree in Fort Berthold and then we found ourselves down in Wakpala somehow and then suddenly we were over in Montana on the Rocky Boys and yet the summer was not even half over. Some people hang on to details when they travel, but we didn't let them bother us and just lived our everyday lives here to there.

I do remember there was this one place with willows, however. I lay under those trees and it was comfortable. So comfortable. The branches bent down all around me like a tent or a stable. And quiet, it was quiet, even though there was a dance close enough so I could see it going on. It was not too still, or too windy either, that day. When the dust rises up and hangs in the air around the dancers like that I feel comfortable. Stephan was asleep. Later on he woke up and we started driving again. We were somewhere in Montana, or maybe on the Blood Reserve, it could have been anywhere. Anyway, it was where we met the girl.

All her hair was in buns around her ears, that's the first thing I saw. She was alongside the road with her arm out so we stopped. That girl was short, so short her lumbershirt looked comical on her, like a nightgown. She had jeans on and fancy moccasins and she carried a little suitcase.

"Hop in," says Stephan. So she climbs in between us.

"We'll take you home," I says, "Where do you live?"

"Chicken," she says.

"Where's that?" I ask her.

"Alaska."

"Okay," Stephan says, and we drive.

We got up there and never wanted to leave. The sun doesn't truly set there in summer and the night is more a soft dusk. You might doze off, sometimes, but before you know it you're up again, like an animal in nature. You never feel like you have to sleep hard or put away the world. And things would grow up there. One day just dirt or moss, the next day flowers and long grass. The girl's family really took to us. They fed us and put us up. We had our own tent to live in by their house and the kids would be in and out of there all day and night.

One night the girl, Susy (she had another, longer name, but they called her Susy for short), came in to visit us. We sat around in the tent talking of this thing and that. It was getting darker by that time and the cold was even getting just a little mean. I told Susy it was time for us to go. She stood up on a chair. "You never seen my hair," she said. That was true. She was standing on a chair, but still, when she un-clipped her buns the hair reached all the way to the ground. Our eyes opened. You couldn't tell how much hair she had when it was rolled up so neatly. Then Stephan did something funny. He went up to the chair and said, "Jump on my shoul-ders." So she did that and her hair reached down past Ste-phan's waist and he started twirling, this way and that, so her hair was flung out from side to side. "I always wondered what it was like to have long pretty hair," Stephan says! Well, we laughed. It was a funny sight, the way he did it. The next morning we got up and took leave of those people.

On to greener pastures, as they say. It was down through Spokane and across Idaho then Montana, and very soon we were racing the weather right along under the Canadian bor-der through Columbus, Des Lacs, and then we were in Botti-neau County and soon home. We'd made most of the trip, that summer, without putting up the car hood at all. We got home just in time, it turned out, for the Army to remember Stephan had signed up to join it.

I don't wonder that the Army was so glad to get Stephan that they turned him into a Marine. He was built like a brick outhouse anyway. We liked to tease him that they really wanted him for his Indian nose, though. He had a nose big and sharp as a hatchet. He had a nose like the nose on Red Tomahawk, the Indian who killed Sitting Bull, whose profile is on signs all along the North Dakota highways. Stephan went off to training camp, came home once during Christmas, then the next thing you know we got an overseas letter from Stephan. It was 1968, and he was stationed in Khe Sanh. I wrote him back several times. I kept him informed all about the car. Most of the time I had it up on blocks in the yard or half taken apart because that long trip wore out so much of it although, I must say, it gave us a beautiful performance when we needed it.

It was at least two years before Stephan came home again. They didn't want him back for a while, I guess, so he stayed on after Christmas. In those two years, I'd put his car into almost perfect shape. I always thought of it as his car, while he was gone, though when he left he said, "Now it's yours," and even threw me his key. "Thanks for the extra key," I said. "I'll put it up in your drawer just in case I need it." He laughed.

When he came home, though, Stephan was very different, and I'll say this, the change was no good. You could hardly expect him to change for the better; I know this. But he was quiet, so quiet, and never comfortable sitting still anywhere but always up and moving around. I thought back to times we'd sat still for whole afternoons, never moving, just shifting our weight along the ground, talking to whoever sat with us, watching things. He'd always had a joke then, too, and now you couldn't get him to laugh, or when he did it was more the sound of a man choking, a sound that stopped up the laughter in the throats of other people around him. They got to leaving him alone most of the time and I didn't blame them. It was a fact, Stephan was jumpy and mean.

I'd bought a color TV set for my mother and the kids while Stephan was away. (Money still came very easy.) I was sorry I'd ever bought it, though, because of Stephan, and I was also sorry I'd bought color because with black-and-white the pictures seem older and farther away. But what are you going to do? He sat in front of it, watching it, and that was the only time he was completely still. But it was the kind of stillness that you see in a rabbit when it freezes and before it will bolt. He was not comfortable. He sat in his chair gripping the armrests with all his might as if the chair itself was moving at a high speed, and if he let go at all he would rocket forward and maybe crash right through the set.

Once I was in the same room and I heard his teeth click at something. I looked over and he'd bitten through his lip. Blood was going down his chin. I tell you right then I wanted to smash that tube to pieces. I went over to it but Stephan must have known what I was up to. He rushed from his chair and shoved me out of the way, against the wall. I told myself he didn't know what he was doing.

My mother came in, turned the set off real quiet, and told us she had made something for supper. So we went and sat down. There was still blood going down Stephan's chin but he didn't notice it, and no one said anything even though every time he took a bite of his bread his blood fell onto it until he was eating his own blood mixed in with the food.

We talked, while Stephan was not around, about what was going to happen to him. There were no Indian doctors on the reservation, no medicine people, and my mother was afraid if we brought him to a regular hospital they would keep him. "No way would we get him there in the first place," I

said, "so let's just forget about it." Then I thought about the
car. Stephan had not even looked at the car since he'd gotten
home, though like I said, it was in tip-top condition and
ready to drive.

One night Stephan was off somewhere. I took myself a
hammer. I went out to that car and I did a number on its
underside. Whacked it up. Bent the tailpipe double. Ripped
the muffler loose. By the time I was done with the car it
looked worse than any typical Indian car that has been driven
all its life on reservation roads which they always say are like
government promises — full of holes. It just about hurt me,
I'll tell you that! I threw dirt in the carburetor and I ripped
all the electric tape off the seats. I made it look just as beat
up as I could. Then I sat back, and I waited for Stephan to
find it.

Still, it took him over a month. That was all right because
it was just getting warm enough, not melting but warm
enough, to work outside, when he did find it.

"Marty," he says, walking in one day, "that red car looks
like shit."

"Well it's old," I says. "You got to expect that."

"No way!" says Stephan. "That car's a classic! But you
went and ran the piss right out of it, Marty, and you know it
don't deserve that. I kept that car in A-1 shape. You don't
remember. You're too young. But when I left, that car was
running like a watch. Now I don't even know if I can get it
to start again, let alone get it anywhere near its old condition."

"Well, you try," I said, like I was getting mad, "but I say
it's a piece of junk."

Then I walked out before he could realize I knew he'd
strung together more than six words at once.

*   *   *

After that I thought he'd freeze himself to death working on that vehicle. I mean he was out there all day and at night he rigged up a little lamp, ran a cord out the window, and had himself some light to see by while he worked. He was better than he had been before, but that's still not saying much. It was easier for him to do the things the rest of us did. He ate more slowly and didn't jump up and down during the meal to get this or that or look out the window. I put my hand in the back of the TV set, I admit, and fiddled around with it good so that it was almost impossible now to get a clear picture. He didn't look at it very often. He was always out with that car or going off to get parts for it. By the time it was really melting outside, he had it fixed.

I had been feeling down in the dumps about Stephan around this time. We had always been together before. Stephan and Marty. But he was such a loner now I didn't know how to take it. So I jumped at the chance one day when Stephan seemed friendly. It's not that he smiled or anything. He just said, "Let's take that old shitbox for a spin." But just the way he said it made me think he could be coming around.

We went out to the car. It was spring. The sun was shining very bright. My little sister Bonita came out and made us stand together for a picture. He leaned his elbow on the red car's windshield and he took his other arm and put it over my shoulder, very carefully, as though it was heavy for him to lift and he didn't want to bring the weight down all at once. "Smile," Bonita said, and he did.

That picture. I never look at it anymore. A few months ago, I don't know why, I got his picture out and tacked it on my wall. I felt good about Stephan at the time, close to him. I felt good having his picture on the wall until one night when I was looking at television. I was a little drunk and stoned. I

looked up at the wall and Stephan was staring at me. I don't
know what it was but his smile had changed. Or maybe it
was gone. All I know is I couldn't stay in the same room with
that picture. I was shaking. I had to get up, close the door,
and go into the kitchen. A little later my friend Rayman
came and we both went back into that room. We put the
picture in a bag and folded the bag over and over and put the
picture way back in the closet.

I still see that picture now, as if it tugs at me, whenever I
pass that closet door. It is very clear in my mind. It was so
sunny that day, Stephan had to squint against the glare. Or
maybe the camera Bonita held flashed like a mirror, blinding
him, before she snapped the picture. My face is right out in
the sun, big and round. But he might have drawn back a little
because the shadows on his face are deep as holes. There are
two shadows curved like little hooks around the ends of his
smile as if to frame it and try to keep it there — that one,
first smile that looked like it might have hurt his face. He
has his field jacket on, and the worn-in clothes he'd come
back in and kept wearing ever since. After Bonita took the
picture and went into the house, we got into the car. There
was a full cooler in the trunk. We started off, east, toward
Pembina and the Red River because Stephan said he wanted
to see the high water.

The trip over there was beautiful. When everything starts
changing, drying up, clearing off, you feel so good it is like
your whole life is starting. And Stephan felt it too. The top
was down and the car hummed like a top. He'd really put it
back in shape, even the tape on the seats was very carefully
put down and glued back in layers. It's not that he smiled
again or even joked or anything while we were driving, but
his face looked to me as if it was clear, more peaceful. It

looked as though he wasn't thinking of anything in particular except the blank fields and windbreaks and houses we were passing.

The river was high and full of winter trash when we got there. The sun was still out, but it was colder by the river. There were still little clumps of dirty snow here and there on the banks. The water hadn't gone over the banks yet, but it would, you could tell. It was just at its limit, hard, swollen, glossy like an old gray scar. We made ourselves a fire, and we sat down and watched the current go. As I watched it I felt something squeezing inside me and tightening and trying to let go all at the same time. I knew I was not just feeling it myself; I knew I was feeling what Stephan was going through at that moment. Except that Marty couldn't stand it, the feeling. I jumped to my feet. I took Stephan by the shoulders and I started shaking him. "Wake up," I says, "wake up, wake up, wake up!" I didn't know what had come over me. I sat down beside him again. His face was totally white, hard, like a stone. Then it broke, like stones break all of the sudden when water boils up inside them.

"I know it," he says. "I know it. I can't help it. It's no use."

We started talking. He said he knew what I'd done with the car that time. It was obvious it had been whacked out of shape and not just neglected. He said he wanted to give the car to me for good now; it was no use. He said he'd fixed it just to give back and I should take it.

"No," I says, "I don't want it."

"That's okay," he says. "You take it."

"I don't want it though," I says back to him and then to emphasize, just to emphasize you understand, I touch his shoulder. He slaps my hand off.

"Take that car," he says.

"No," I say, "make me," I say, and then he grabs my jacket and rips the arm loose. I get mad and push him backwards, off the log. He jumps up and bowls me over. We go down in a clinch and come up swinging hard, for all we're worth, with our fists. He socks my jaw so hard I feel like it swings loose. Then I'm at his rib cage and land a good one under his chin so his head snaps back. He's dazzled. He looks at me and I look at him and then his eyes are full of tears and blood and he's crying I think at first. But no, he's laughing. "Ha! Ha!" he says. "Ha! Ha! Take good care of it!"

"Okay," I says, "Okay no problem. Ha! Ha!"

I can't help it and I start laughing too. My face feels fat and strange and after a while I get a beer from the cooler in the trunk and when I hand it to Stephan he takes his shirt and wipes my germs off. "Hoof and mouth disease," he says. For some reason this cracks me up and so we're really laughing for a while then, and then we drink all the rest of the beers one by one and throw them in the river and see how far the current takes them, how fast, before they fill up and sink.

"I'm an Indian!" he shouts after a while.

"Whoo I'm on the lovepath! I'm out for loving!"

I think it's the old Stephan. He jumps up then and starts swinging his legs out from the knees like a fancydancer, then he's down doing something between a grouse dance and a bunny hop, no kind of dance I ever saw before but neither has anyone else on all this green growing earth. He's wild. He wants to pitch whoopee! He's up and at 'em and all over. All this time I'm laughing so hard, so hard my belly is getting tied up in a knot.

"Got to cool me off!" he shouts all of the sudden. Then he runs over to the river and jumps in.

There's boards and other things in the current. It's so high. No sound comes from the river after the splash he makes so

I run right over. I look around. It's dark. I see he's halfway across the water already and I know he didn't swim there but the current took him. It's far. I hear his voice, though, very clearly across it.

"My boots are filling," he says.

He says this in a normal voice, like he just noticed and he doesn't know what to think of it. Then he's gone. A branch comes by. Another branch. And then there's only the water, the sound of it going and running and going and running and running.

By the time I get out of the river, off the snag I pulled myself onto, the sun is down. I walk back to the car, turn on the high beams, and drive it up the bank. I put it in first gear and then I take my foot off the clutch. I get out, close the door, and watch it plow softly into the water. The headlights reach in as they go down, searching, still lighted even after the water swirls over the back end. I wait. The wires short out. It is all finally dark. I tell myself, "Marty, you must walk home. They are waiting."

The Man I Killed

from *The Things They Carried*

Tim O'Brien

His jaw was in his throat, his upper lip and teeth were gone, his one eye was shut, his other eye was a star-shaped hole, his eyebrows were thin and arched like a woman's, his nose was undamaged, there was a slight tear at the lobe of one ear, his clean black hair was swept upward into a cowlick at the rear of the skull, his forehead was lightly freckled, his fingernails were clean, the skin at his left cheek was peeled back in three ragged strips, his right cheek was smooth and hairless, there was a butterfly on his chin, his neck was open to the spinal cord and the blood there was thick and shiny and it was this wound that had killed him. He lay face-up in the center of the trail, a slim, dead, almost dainty young man. He had bony legs, a narrow waist, long shapely fingers. His chest was sunken and poorly muscled — a scholar, maybe. His wrists were the wrists of a child. He wore a black shirt, black pajama pants, a gray ammunition belt, a gold ring on the third finger of his right hand. His rubber sandals had been blown off. One lay beside him, the other a few meters up the trail. He had been born, maybe, in 1946 in the village of My Khe near the central coastline of Quang Ngai Province, where his parents farmed, and where his family had lived for several centuries, and where, during the time of the French, his father and two uncles and many neighbors had joined in the struggle for independence. He was not a Communist. He was a citizen and a soldier. In the village of My Khe, as in all of Quang Ngai, patriotic resistance had the force of tradition, which was partly the force of legend, and from his earliest boyhood the man I killed had listened to stories about the heroic Trung sisters and Tran Hung Dao's famous rout of the Mongols and Le Loi's final victory against the Chinese at Tot Dong. He had been taught that to defend the land was a man's highest duty and highest privilege. He accepted this. It was never open to question. Secretly, though, it also frightened him. He was not a fighter. His health was poor, his body small and frail. He liked books. He wanted someday to be a teacher of mathematics. At night, lying on his mat, he could not picture himself doing the brave things his father had done, or his uncles, or the heroes of the stories. He hoped in his heart that he would never be tested. He hoped the Americans would go away. Soon, he hoped. He kept hoping and hoping, always, even when he was asleep.

"Oh, man, you fuckin' trashed the fucker," Azar said. "You scrambled his sorry self, look at that, you *did*, you laid him out like Shredded fuckin' Wheat."

"Go away," Kiowa said.

"I'm just saying the truth. Like oatmeal."

"Go," Kiowa said.

"Okay, then, I take it back," Azar said. He started to move away, then stopped and said, "Rice Krispies, you know? On the dead test, this particular individual gets A-plus."

Smiling at this, he shrugged and walked up the trail toward the village behind the trees.

Kiowa kneeled down.

"Just forget that crud," he said. He opened up his canteen

and held it out for a while and then sighed and pulled it away. "No sweat, man. What else could you do?"

Later, Kiowa said, "I'm serious. Nothing *anybody* could do. Come on, Tim, stop staring."

The trail junction was shaded by a row of trees and tall brush. The slim young man lay with his legs in the shade. His jaw was in his throat. His one eye was shut and the other was a star-shaped hole.

Kiowa glanced at the body.

"All right, let me ask a question," he said. "You want to trade places with him? Turn it all upside down — you *want* that? I mean, be honest."

The star-shaped hole was red and yellow. The yellow part seemed to be getting wider, spreading out at the center of the star. The upper lip and gum and teeth were gone. The man's head was cocked at a wrong angle, as if loose at the neck, and the neck was wet with blood.

"Think it over," Kiowa said.

Then later he said, "Tim, it's a *war*. The guy wasn't Heidi — he had a weapon, right? It's a tough thing, for sure, but you got to cut out that staring."

Then he said, "Maybe you better lie down a minute."

Then after a long empty time he said, "Take it slow. Just go wherever the spirit takes you."

The butterfly was making its way along the young man's forehead, which was spotted with small dark freckles. The nose was undamaged. The skin on the right cheek was smooth and fine-grained and hairless. Frail-looking, delicately boned, the young man had never wanted to be a soldier and in his heart had feared that he would perform badly in battle. Even as a boy growing up in the village of My Khe, he had often worried about this. He imagined covering his head and lying in a deep hole and closing his eyes and not moving until the war was over. He had no stomach for violence. He loved mathematics. His eyebrows were thin and arched like a woman's, and at school the boys sometimes teased him about how pretty he was, the arched eyebrows and long shapely fingers, and on the playground they would mimic a woman's walk and make fun of his smooth skin and his love for mathe- matics. He could not make himself fight them. He often wanted to, but he was afraid, and this increased his shame. If he could not fight little boys, he thought, how could he ever become a soldier and fight the Americans with their air- planes and helicopters and bombs? It did not seem possible. In the presence of his father and uncles, he pretended to look for- ward to doing his patriotic duty, which was also a privilege, but at night he prayed with his mother that the war might end soon. Beyond anything else, he was afraid of disgracing him- self, and therefore his family and village. But all he could do, he thought, was wait and pray and try not to grow up too fast.

"Listen to me," Kiowa said. "You feel terrible, I know that."

Then he said, "Okay, maybe I *don't* know."

Along the trail there were small blue flowers shaped like bells. The young man's head was wrenched sideways, not quite facing the flowers, and even in the shade a single blade of sunlight sparkled against the buckle of his ammunition belt. The left cheek was peeled back in three ragged strips. The wounds at his neck had not yet clotted, which made him seem animate even in death, the blood still spreading out across his shirt.

Kiowa shook his head.

There was some silence before he said, "Stop *staring*."

The young man's fingernails were clean. There was a slight tear at the lobe of one ear, a sprinkling of blood on the forearm. He wore a gold ring on the third finger of his right hand. His chest was sunken and poorly muscled — a scholar, maybe. For years, despite his family's poverty, the man I killed had been determined to continue his education in mathematics. The means for this were arranged, perhaps, through the village liberation cadres, and in 1964 the young man began attending classes at the university in Saigon, where he avoided politics and paid attention to the problems of calculus. He devoted himself to his studies. He spent his nights alone, wrote romantic poems in his journal, took pleasure in the grace and beauty of differential equations. The war, he knew, would finally take him, but for the time being he would not let himself think about it. He had stopped praying; instead, now, he waited. And as he waited, in his final year at the university, he fell in love with a classmate, a girl of seventeen, who one day told him that his wrists were like the wrists of a child, so small and delicate, and who admired his narrow waist and the cowlick that rose up like a bird's tail at the back of his head. She liked his quiet manner; she laughed at his freckles and bony legs. One evening, perhaps, they exchanged gold rings.

Now one eye was a star.

"You okay?" Kiowa said.

The body lay almost entirely in shade. There were gnats at the mouth, little flecks of pollen drifting above the nose. The butterfly was gone. The bleeding had stopped except for the neck wounds.

Kiowa picked up the rubber sandals, clapping off the dirt, then bent down to search the body. He found a pouch of rice, a comb, a fingernail clipper, a few soiled piasters, a snapshot of a young woman standing in front of a parked motorcycle. Kiowa placed these items in his rucksack along with the gray ammunition belt and rubber sandals.

Then he squatted down.

"I'll tell you the straight truth," he said. "The guy was dead the second he stepped on the trail. Understand me? We all had him zeroed. A good kill — weapon, ammunition, everything." Tiny beads of sweat glistened at Kiowa's forehead. His eyes moved from the sky to the dead man's body to the knuckles of his own hands. "So listen, you have to pull your shit together. Can't just sit here all day."

Later he said, "Understand?"

Then he said, "Five minutes, Tim. Five more minutes and we're moving out."

The one eye did a funny twinkling trick, red to yellow. His head was wrenched sideways, as if loose at the neck, and the dead young man seemed to be staring at some distant object beyond the bell-shaped flowers along the trail. The blood at the neck had gone to a deep purplish black. Clean fingernails, clean hair — he had been a soldier for only a single day. After his years at the university, the man I killed returned with his new wife to the village of My Khe, where he enlisted as a common rifleman with the 48th Vietcong Battalion. He knew he would die quickly. He knew he would see a flash of light. He knew he would fall dead and wake up in the stories of his village and people.

Kiowa covered the body with a poncho.

"Hey, Tim, you're looking better," he said. "No doubt about it. All you needed was time — some mental R&R."

Then he said, "Man, I'm sorry."

Then later he said, "Why not talk about it?"

Then he said, "Come on, man, talk."

He was a slim, dead, almost dainty young man of about twenty. He lay with one leg bent beneath him, his jaw in his throat, his face neither expressive nor inexpressive. One eye was shut. The other was a star-shaped hole.

"Talk to me," Kiowa said.

Ambush

from *The Things They Carried*

Tim O'Brien

When she was nine, my daughter Kathleen asked if I had ever killed anyone. She knew about the war; she knew I'd been a soldier. "You keep writing these war stories," she said, "so I guess you must've killed somebody." It was a difficult moment, but I did what seemed right, which was to say, "Of course not," and then to take her onto my lap and hold her for a while. Someday, I hope, she'll ask again. But here I want to pretend she's a grown-up. I want to tell her exactly what happened, or what I remember happening, and then I want to say to her that as a little girl she was absolutely right. This is why I keep writing war stories:

He was a short, slender young man of about twenty. I was afraid of him — afraid of something — and as he passed me on the trail I threw a grenade that exploded at his feet and killed him.

Or to go back:

Shortly after midnight we moved into the ambush site outside My Khe. The whole platoon was there, spread out in the dense brush along the trail, and for five hours nothing at all happened. We were working in two-man teams — one man

on guard while the other slept, switching off every two hours
— and I remember it was still dark when Kiowa shook me
awake for the final watch. The night was foggy and hot. For
the first few moments I felt lost, not sure about directions,
groping for my helmet and weapon. I reached out and found
three grenades and lined them up in front of me; the pins
had already been straightened for quick throwing. And then
for maybe half an hour I kneeled there and waited. Very
gradually, in tiny slivers, dawn began to break through the
fog, and from my position in the brush I could see ten or
fifteen meters up the trail. The mosquitoes were fierce. I remember slapping at them, wondering if I should wake up
Kiowa and ask for some repellent, then thinking it was a bad
idea, then looking up and seeing the young man come out of
the fog. He wore black clothing and rubber sandals and a
gray ammunition belt. His shoulders were slightly stooped, his
head cocked to the side as if listening for something. He
seemed at ease. He carried his weapon in one hand, muzzle
down, moving without any hurry up the center of the trail.
There was no sound at all — none that I can remember. In
a way, it seemed, he was part of the morning fog, or my
own imagination, but there was also the reality of what was
happening in my stomach. I had already pulled the pin on
a grenade. I had come up to a crouch. It was entirely auto-
matic. I did not hate the young man; I did not see him as
the enemy; I did not ponder issues of morality or politics or
military duty. I crouched and kept my head low. I tried to
swallow whatever was rising from my stomach, which tasted
like lemonade, something fruity and sour. I was terrified.
There were no thoughts about killing. The grenade was to
make him go away — just evaporate — and I leaned back
and felt my mind go empty and then felt it fill up again. I
had already thrown the grenade before telling myself to throw

it. The brush was thick and I had to lob it high, not aiming, and I remember the grenade seeming to freeze above me for an instant, as if a camera had clicked, and I remember ducking down and holding my breath and seeing little wisps of fog rise from the earth. The grenade bounced once and rolled across the trail. I did not hear it, but there must've been a sound, because the young man dropped his weapon and began to run, just two or three quick steps, then he hesitated, swiveling to his right, and he glanced down at the grenade and tried to cover his head but never did. It occurred to me then that he was about to die. I wanted to warn him. The grenade made a popping noise — not soft but not loud either — not what I'd expected — and there was a puff of dust and smoke — a small white puff — and the young man seemed to jerk upward as if pulled by invisible wires. He fell on his back. His rubber sandals had been blown off. There was no wind. He lay at the center of the trail, his right leg bent beneath him, his one eye shut, his other eye a huge star-shaped hole.

It was not a matter of live or die. There was no real peril. Almost certainly the young man would have passed by. And it will always be that way.

Later, I remember, Kiowa tried to tell me that the man would've died anyway. He told me that it was a good kill, that I was a soldier and this was a war, that I should shape up and stop staring and ask myself what the dead man would've done if things were reversed.

None of it mattered. The words seemed far too complicated. All I could do was gape at the fact of the young man's body.

Even now I haven't finished sorting it out. Sometimes I forgive myself, other times I don't. In the ordinary hours of life I try not to dwell on it, but now and then, when I'm reading a newspaper or just sitting alone in a room, I'll look up and see the young man coming out of the morning fog. I'll watch him walk toward me, his shoulders slightly stooped, his head cocked to the side, and he'll pass within a few yards of me and suddenly smile at some secret thought and then continue up the trail to where it bends back into the fog.

from

I Know Why the Caged Bird Sings

Maya Angelou

For nearly a year, I sopped around the house, the Store, the school, and the church, like an old biscuit, dirty and inedible. Then I met, or rather got to know, the lady who threw me my first lifeline.

Mrs. Bertha Flowers was the aristocrat of Black Stamps. She had the grace of control to appear warm in the coldest weather, and on the Arkansas summer days it seemed she had a private breeze which swirled around, cooling her. She was thin without the taut look of wiry people, and her printed voile dresses and flowered hats were as right for her as denim overalls for a farmer. She was our side's answer to the richest white woman in town.

Her skin was a rich black that would have peeled like a plum if snagged, but then no one would have thought of getting close enough to Mrs. Flowers to ruffle her dress, let alone snag her skin. She didn't encourage familiarity. She wore gloves too.

I don't think I ever saw Mrs. Flowers laugh, but she smiled often. A slow widening of her thin black lips to show even, small white teeth, then the slow effortless closing. When she chose to smile on me, I always wanted to thank her. The action was so graceful and inclusively benign.

She was one of the few gentlewomen I have ever known, and has remained throughout my life the measure of what a human being can be.

Momma had a strange relationship with her. Most often when she passed on the road in front of the Store, she spoke to Momma in that soft yet carrying voice, "Good day, Mrs. Henderson." Momma responded with "How you, Sister Flowers?"

Mrs. Flowers didn't belong to our church, nor was she Momma's familiar. Why on earth did she insist on calling her Sister Flowers? Shame made me want to hide my face. Mrs. Flowers deserved better than to be called Sister. Then, Momma left out the verb. Why not ask, "How *are* you, *Mrs.* Flowers?" With the unbalanced passion of the young, I hated her for showing her ignorance to Mrs. Flowers. It didn't occur to me for many years that they were as alike as sisters, separated only by formal education.

Although I was upset, neither of the women was in the least shaken by what I thought an unceremonious greeting. Mrs. Flowers would continue her easy gait up the hill to her little bungalow, and Momma kept on shelling peas or doing whatever had brought her to the front porch.

Occasionally, though, Mrs. Flowers would drift off the road and down to the Store and Momma would say to me, "Sister, you go on and play." As I left I would hear the beginning of an intimate conversation. Momma persistently using the wrong verb, or none at all.

"Brother and Sister Wilcox is sho'ly the meanest —" "Is," Momma? "Is"? Oh, please, not "is," Momma, for two or more. But they talked, and from the side of the building where I waited for the ground to open up and swallow me, I heard the soft-voiced Mrs. Flowers and the textured voice of my grandmother merging and melting. They were interrupted from time to time by giggles that must have come from Mrs. Flowers (Momma never giggled in her life). Then she was gone.

She appealed to me because she was like people I had never met personally. Like women in English novels who walked the moors (whatever they were) with their loyal dogs racing at a respectful distance. Like the women who sat in front of roaring fireplaces, drinking tea incessantly from silver trays full of scones and crumpets. Women who walked over the "heath" and read morocco-bound books and had two last names divided by a hyphen. It would be safe to say that she made me proud to be Negro, just by being herself.

She acted just as refined as whitefolks in the movies and books and she was more beautiful, for none of them could have come near that warm color without looking gray by comparison.

It was fortunate that I never saw her in the company of powhitefolks. For since they tend to think of their whiteness as an evenizer, I'm certain that I would have had to hear her spoken to commonly as Bertha, and my image of her would have been shattered like the unmendable Humpty-Dumpty.

One summer afternoon, sweet-milk fresh in my memory, she stopped at the Store to buy provisions. Another Negro woman of her health and age would have been expected to carry the paper sacks home in one hand, but Momma said, "Sister Flowers, I'll send Bailey up to your house with these things."

She smiled that slow dragging smile, "Thank you, Mrs. Henderson. I'd prefer Marguerite, though." My name was beautiful when she said it. "I've been meaning to talk to her, anyway." They gave each other age-group looks.

Momma said, "Well, that's all right then. Sister, go and change your dress. You going to Sister Flowers's."

The chifforobe was a maze. What on earth did one put on to go to Mrs. Flowers' house? I knew I shouldn't put on a Sunday dress. It might be sacrilegious. Certainly not a house dress, since I was already wearing a fresh one. I chose a school dress, naturally. It was formal without suggesting that going to Mrs. Flowers' house was equivalent to attending church.

I trusted myself back into the Store.

"Now, don't you look nice." I had chosen the right thing, for once.

"Mrs. Henderson, you make most of the children's clothes, don't you?"

"Yes, ma'am. Sure do. Store-bought clothes ain't hardly worth the thread it take to stitch them."

"I'll say you do a lovely job, though, so neat. That dress looks professional."

Momma was enjoying the seldom-received compliments. Since everyone we knew (except Mrs. Flowers, of course) could sew competently, praise was rarely handed out for the commonly practiced craft.

"I try, with the help of the Lord, Sister Flowers, to finish the inside just like I does the outside. Come here, Sister."

I had buttoned up the collar and tied the belt, apronlike, in back. Momma told me to turn around. With one hand she pulled the strings and the belt fell free at both sides of my waist. Then her large hands were at my neck, opening the button loops. I was terrified. What was happening?

"Take it off, Sister." She had her hands on the hem of the dress.

"I don't need to see the inside, Mrs. Henderson, I can tell . . ." But the dress was over my head and my arms were stuck in the sleeves. Momma said, "That'll do. See here,

Sister Flowers, I French-seams around the armholes."
Through the cloth film, I saw the shadow approach. "That
makes it last longer. Children these days would bust out of
sheet-metal clothes. They so rough."

"That is a very good job, Mrs. Henderson. You should be
proud. You can put your dress back on, Marguerite."

"No ma'am. Pride is a sin. And 'cording to the Good Book,
it goeth before a fall."

"That's right. So the Bible says. It's a good thing to keep
in mind."

I wouldn't look at either of them. Momma hadn't thought
that taking off my dress in front of Mrs. Flowers would kill
me stone dead. If I had refused, she would have thought I
was trying to be "womanish" and might have remembered St.
Louis. Mrs. Flowers had known that I would be embarrassed
and that was even worse. I picked up the groceries and went
out to wait in the hot sunshine. It would be fitting if I got a
sunstroke and died before they came outside. Just dropped
dead on the slanting porch.

There was a little path beside the rocky road, and Mrs.
Flowers walked in front swinging her arms and picking her
way over the stones.

She said, without turning her head, to me, "I hear you're
doing very good school work, Marguerite, but that it's all
written. The teachers report that they have trouble getting
you to talk in class." We passed the triangular farm on our
left and the path widened to allow us to walk together. I hung
back in the separate unasked and unanswerable questions.

"Come and walk along with me, Marguerite." I couldn't
have refused even if I wanted to. She pronounced my name
so nicely. Or more correctly, she spoke each word with such
clarity that I was certain a foreigner who didn't understand
English could have understood her.

"Now no one is going to make you talk — possibly no one can. But bear in mind, language is man's way of communicating with his fellow man and it is language alone which separates him from the lower animals." That was a totally new idea to me, and I would need time to think about it.

"Your grandmother says you read a lot. Every chance you get. That's good, but not good enough. Words mean more than what is set down on paper. It takes the human voice to infuse them with the shades of deeper meaning."

I memorized the part about the human voice infusing words. It seemed so valid and poetic.

She said she was going to give me some books and that I not only must read them, I must read them aloud. She suggested that I try to make a sentence sound in as many different ways as possible.

"I'll accept no excuse if you return a book to me that has been badly handled." My imagination boggled at the punishment I would deserve if in fact I did abuse a book of Mrs. Flowers'. Death would be too kind and brief.

The odors in the house surprised me. Somehow I had never connected Mrs. Flowers with food or eating or any other common experience of common people. There must have been an outhouse, too, but my mind never recorded it.

The sweet scent of vanilla had met us as she opened the door.

"I made tea cookies this morning. You see, I had planned to invite you for cookies and lemonade so we could have this little chat. The lemonade is in the icebox."

It followed that Mrs. Flowers would have ice on an ordinary day, when most families in our town bought ice late on Saturdays only a few times during the summer to be used in the wooden ice-cream freezers.

She took the bags from me and disappeared through the

kitchen door. I looked around the room that I had never in my wildest fantasies imagined I would see. Browned photographs leered or threatened from the walls and the white, freshly done curtains pushed against themselves and against the wind. I wanted to gobble up the room entire and take it to Bailey, who would help me analyze and enjoy it.

"Have a seat, Marguerite. Over there by the table." She carried a platter covered with a tea towel. Although she warned that she hadn't tried her hand at baking sweets for some time, I was certain that like everything else about her the cookies would be perfect.

They were flat round wafers, slightly browned on the edges and butter-yellow in the center. With the cold lemonade they were sufficient for childhood's lifelong diet. Remembering my manners, I took nice little lady-like bites off the edges. She said she had made them expressly for me and that she had a few in the kitchen that I could take home to my brother. So I jammed one whole cake in my mouth and the rough crumbs scratched the insides of my jaws, and if I hadn't had to swallow, it would have been a dream come true.

As I ate she began the first of what we later called "my lessons in living." She said that I must always be intolerant of ignorance but understanding of illiteracy. That some people, unable to go to school, were more educated and even more intelligent than college professors. She encouraged me to listen carefully to what country people called mother wit. That in those homely sayings was couched the collective wisdom of generations.

When I finished the cookies she brushed off the table and brought a thick, small book from the bookcase. I had read *A Tale of Two Cities* and found it up to my standards as a romantic novel. She opened the first page and I heard poetry for the first time in my life.

"It was the best of times and the worst of times . . ." Her voice slid in and curved down through and over the words. She was nearly singing. I wanted to look at the pages. Were they the same that I had read? Or were there notes, music, lined on the pages, as in a hymn book? Her sounds began cascading gently. I knew from listening to a thousand preachers that she was nearing the end of her reading, and I hadn't really heard, heard to understand, a single word.

"How do you like that?"

It occurred to me that she expected a response. The sweet vanilla flavor was still on my tongue and her reading was a wonder in my ears. I had to speak.

I said, "Yes, ma'am." It was the least I could do, but it was the most also.

"There's one more thing. Take this book of poems and memorize one for me. Next time you pay me a visit, I want you to recite."

I have tried often to search behind the sophistication of years for the enchantment I so easily found in those gifts. The essence escapes but its aura remains. To be allowed, no, invited, into the private lives of strangers, and to share their joys and fears, was a chance to exchange the Southern bitter wormwood for a cup of mead with Beowulf or a hot cup of tea and milk with Oliver Twist. When I said aloud, "It is a far, far better thing that I do, than I have ever done . . ." tears of love filled my eyes at my selflessness.

Poesía a la amistad

José Martí

Cultivo una rosa blanca
en junio como en enero
para el amigo sincero,
que me da su mano franca
y para el cruel quel me arranca
el corazón con que vivo
gardos ni ortiga cultivo
cultivo una rosa blanca.

Poetry of Friendship

I cultivate a white rose
In June as in January
For a genuine friend,
That gives his unadorned hand
And for the cruelty that plucks
This heart that lives within
I do not cultivate gardenias nor weeds
I cultivate a white rose.

Translated by Raúl Niño

Notes on the Authors

Maya Angelou, poet, musician, and performer, has written a series of great personal narratives, beginning with the now classic *I Know Why the Caged Bird Sings,* which James Baldwin called "a Biblical study of life in the midst of death." What led to the silence in this excerpt was a rape at age eight.

Toni Cade Bambara is a well-known civil rights activist and professor of English and African American studies. Her books include the widely read *The Salt Eaters,* which received the American Book Award in 1981, and a collection of short stories, *Gorilla, My Love,* from which "Raymond's Run" is taken.

Ray Bradbury based *Dandelion Wine* on his own midwestern boyhood. He grew up in Waukegan, Illinois; Arizona; and Los Angeles. Some of his best-loved books are the science fiction *The Martian Chronicles,* the futurist *Fahrenheit 451,* and the short-story collection *Something Wicked This Way Comes.*

Martha Brooks is a singer, writer, and teacher from Winnipeg, Canada. Her book *Paradise Café and Other Stories* was chosen by the American Library Association as a Best Book for Young Adults. Her latest novel, *Two Moons in August,* is about love and friendship.

Sandra Cisneros was born and grew up in Chicago, the daughter of a Mexican father and a Mexican-American mother. Her book *The House on Mango Street* is a series of lyrical stories about coming of age as a Chicana, caught between the richness of her immigrant culture and the need to find her own place as an individual woman. *Woman Hollering Creek* is her latest, critically acclaimed collection. She now lives in San Antonio, Texas.

Louise Erdrich grew up in Wahpeton, North Dakota, a member of the Turtle Mountain Band of Chippewa. She lives with her husband, writer Michael Dorris, and their children in New Hampshire. A slightly altered version of "The Red Convertible" appeared in *Love Medicine*, the first of a series of poetic, unsparing books about life on and off the reservation.

Isabel Huggan was born in Canada and lives in Ottawa with her husband and daughter. "Celia Behind Me" is from her acclaimed collection *The Elizabeth Stories*, a book of connected stories that reveal surprising truths about growing up. It is currently being made into a feature film. Her stories have been included in *Best Canadian Stories*.

Langston Hughes, a leading figure of the Harlem Renaissance in the 1920s, continues to be widely read as a poet and story writer. The first volume of his autobiography is *The Big Sea*.

Gish Jen wrote *Typical American*, a touching, funny adult novel about the Chinese-American immigrant experience. Her short stories have appeared in numerous anthologies and magazines, including *The Best American Short Stories*, 1988.

Carson McCullers wrote "Sucker" shortly after graduating from high school. She was twenty-two when her first novel, *The Heart Is a Lonely Hunter*, was published. Born in Georgia, her works are rooted in the South and include *The Member of the Wedding* and *The Ballad of the Sad Café*. Many of her most beloved books are about the pain of unrequited love.

José Martí was a Cuban poet (1853–1895), revolutionary in his politics and in his writing, dedicated to Cuba's struggle for independence from Spain. *"Poesía a la amistad"* ("Poetry of Friendship") is a version of a poem originally published in his most famous anthology, *Versos Sencillos (Plain Poems)*, 1891, written while he lived in exile in the United States. His journalism and his poetry celebrate friendship, justice, and freedom.

Raúl Niño is a Chicago poet, author of the collection *Breathing Light*, published in 1991 by March/Abrazo Press.

Joyce Carol Oates grew up in the country outside Lockport, in western New York. She went to elementary school in a one-room schoolhouse.

A prolific and celebrated writer, she lives with her husband in Detroit. Her astonishing story included here, "Where Are You Going, Where Have You Been?," has been made into the movie *Smooth Talk*, starring Treat Williams.

Tim O'Brien grew up in Minnesota, attended Macalester College and Harvard University, and served as a foot soldier in Vietnam. He is the author of *Going after Cacciato*. The haunting stories in *The Things They Carried* are told in O'Brien's own voice, both poetic and casual, as a twenty-three-year-old foot soldier and as an older writer remembering.

Judith Ortiz-Cofer was born in Puerto Rico. In *Silent Dancing: A Partial Remembrance of a Puerto Rican Childhood*, she blends autobiography and poetry, talking about moving back and forth between the island and the states. She captures the intimacy and the strangeness of being caught between two cultures.

Richard Peck grew up in Decatur, Illinois, and now lives in New York City. His witty, poignant novels include *Father Figure* and *Remembering the Good Times*. He won the 1990 Author Achievement Award given by *School Library Journal* and the Young Adult Services Division of the American Library Association and the 1990 NCTE/ALAN Award.

John Updike is one of the most famous living American writers. He grew up in Shillington, Pennsylvania. Along with his many works of fiction, he has written an autobiography, *Self-Consciousness: A Memoir*. Perhaps his most acclaimed novel is *Rabbit, Run*. He writes regularly for *The New Yorker* and now lives in Massachusetts.

Tobias Wolff, in his candid, beautiful memoir *This Boy's Life*, remembers himself growing up in the Seattle area in the 1950s with the stepfather he hated and the mother he loved. He was a liar and a thief, wild and ugly at times; yet he wished he weren't such a mess and he dreamed that he was a scholar-athlete, a success. "The human heart is a dark forest," Wolff says.

Acknowledgments

Angelou, Maya: from *I Know Why the Caged Bird Sings*, by Maya Angelou, copyright © 1969 by Maya Angelou. Reprinted by permission of Random House, Inc.

Bambara, Toni Cade: "Raymond's Run," published with the permission of the author, copyright © 1972, 1973, 1981, 1983, 1992.

Bradbury, Ray: "Good Grief," from *Dandelion Wine*, reprinted by permission of Don Congdon Associates, Inc. Copyright 1953, renewed 1981 by Ray Bradbury.

Brooks, Martha: "A Boy and His Dog," by Martha Brooks, from *Paradise Café and Other Stories* (Thistledown Press, 1988), used with permission. From *Paradise Café*, by Martha Brooks, copyright © 1988 by Martha Brooks. By permission of Little, Brown and Company.

Cisneros, Sandra: "My Lucy Friend Who Smells Like Corn," from *Woman Hollering Creek*, copyright © 1991 by Sandra Cisneros. Published in the United States by Vintage Books, a division of Random House, Inc., New York, and simultaneously in Canada by Random House of Canada, Ltd., Toronto. Reprinted by permission of Susan Bergholz Literary Services.

Ortiz-Cofer, Judith: "American History," first published in *Iguana Dreams: New Latino Fiction*, Harper Perennial, 1992. Reprinted by permission of the author.

Erdrich, Louise: "The Red Convertible," first published in the *Mississippi Valley Review*. Copyright © 1981 by Louise Erdrich. Reprinted by permission of the author.

169

Huggan, Isabel: "Celia Behind Me," from *The Elizabeth Stories*, by Isabel Huggan, copyright © 1984 by Isabel Huggan. Used by permission of Oberon Press and the author. Used by permission of Viking Penguin, a division of Penguin Books USA Inc.

Hughes, Langston: "Poem," from *The Dream Keeper and Other Poems*, by Langston Hughes, copyright 1932 by Alfred A. Knopf, Inc., and renewed 1960 by Langston Hughes. Reprinted by permission of the publisher.

Jen, Gish: "What Means Switch," copyright © 1990 by Gish Jen. First published in *The Atlantic*. Reprinted by permission of the author.

McCullers, Carson: "Sucker," from *The Mortgaged Heart*, by Carson McCullers, copyright 1940, 1941, 1942, 1945, 1948, 1949, 1953, © 1956, 1959, 1963, 1967, 1971 by Floria V. Lasky, Executrix of the Estate of Carson McCullers. Reprinted by permission of Houghton Mifflin Company. All rights reserved.

Oates, Joyce Carol: "Where Are You Going? Where Have You Been?," copyright © 1970 by Joyce Carol Oates. Reprinted by permission of John Hawkins & Associates, Inc.

O'Brien, Tim: "The Man I Killed" and "Ambush," from *The Things They Carried*, by Tim O'Brien, copyright © 1990 by Tim O'Brien. Reprinted by permission of Houghton Mifflin Co./Seymour Lawrence. All rights reserved.

Peck, Richard: "Priscilla and the Wimps," copyright © 1978 by Richard Peck. First published in *Sixteen* (Donald Gallo, ed.), by Delacorte Press. All rights reserved. Used with permission.

Updike, John: "The Alligators," from *The Same Door*, by John Updike, copyright © 1958 by John Updike. Reprinted by permission of Alfred A. Knopf, Inc. Originally appeared in *The New Yorker*.

Wolff, Tobias: from *This Boy's Life*, by Tobias Wolff, copyright © 1989 by Tobias Wolff. Used by permission of the Atlantic Monthly Press.